PRAISE FOR VIOLET

"Saturated with feeling."
    —*STAR TRIBUNE*

"Shin delivers another meticulous, haunting characterization of an isolated young woman in crisis."
    —*BOOKLIST*, starred review

"With sensuous prose intuitively translated by Hur, Shin vividly captures San's tragic failure to connect with others. This is hard to put down."
    —*PUBLISHERS WEEKLY*

"A shimmering text that blends stark violence with delicate, considered language, preserving, with tender attention, a woman rejected and erased by society."
    —*ASYMPTOTE*

"A novel built on the proximity of beauty and violence. . . . Shin has an intense feeling for place, and an ability to bring it alive not as mere setting but as intensely felt imaginative terrain."
    —*THE GUARDIAN*

"The beauty of Kyung-Sook Shin's prose is in its expert weave of immersion, precision, and surprise. San represents so many women whose stories are never told."
    —WEIKE WANG, author of *Joan Is Okay*

"Mesmerizing, dreamlike, and prescient."
    —SHARLENE TEO, author of *Ponti*

"*Violets* is an aching, atmospheric novel about grief and longing. Oh San, our main character, navigates a life of haunting loneliness and yet she finds tender moments of true beauty. In this slim and powerful book, Kyung-Sook Shin deftly explores the violence of life—of shedding childhood, of becoming a woman, of searching for identity in a shifting world. A beautiful translation by Anton Hur. Go read this book!"
    —CRYSTAL HANA KIM, author of *If You Leave Me*

"Darkly beautiful, *Violets* explores the toll of abandonment and the relentless marginalization of a helpless young woman. The protagonist, San, shivers with insecurity and loneliness but still dares, briefly, to dream of friendship and a normal life. Shin writes of the cruelty and dangers of disempowerment, and an ensuing spiral of despair."

   —FRANCES CHA, author of *If I Had Your Face*

"*Violets* is a moving delve into a lonely psyche, with writing raw and sophisticated, tenderhearted and clear-eyed. Vividly translated by Anton Hur, Kyung-Sook Shin's novel is also an intimate, sideways portrait of Seoul through the eyes of a rural outsider who roams the bright lights and big city, not in pursuit of ambitious dreams, but seeking care and human touch."

   —YZ CHIN, author of *Edge Case*

"Kyung-Sook Shin has a way of seeing past the smooth surface of societal appearance and into the fragile, obscure psychological space that lies just beneath, where her characters ache in ways that feel both recognizable and possessed of deep insight. I don't know if I've ever read a book that so masterfully captures the subtle desperation of seeking a desire that can be your own in a fast-changing world."

   —ALEXANDRA KLEEMAN,
   author of *Something New Under the Sun*

"A subtle, deep, unique work of true literature."

   —DEFNE SUMAN, author of *The Silence of Scheherazade*

"*Violets* depicts the brutal struggle to construct one's own narrative amid a vicious cycle where the workings of money and authority are opaque, and one must mold herself to whatever opportunity is allotted."

   —BONNIE HUIE, translator of *Notes of a Crocodile*

VIOLETS

KYUNG-SOOK SHIN

TRANSLATED FROM THE KOREAN BY ANTON HUR

THE FEMINIST PRESS
AT THE CITY UNIVERSITY OF NEW YORK
NEW YORK CITY

Published in 2022 by the Feminist Press
at the City University of New York
The Graduate Center
365 Fifth Avenue, Suite 5406
New York, NY 10016

feministpress.org

First Feminist Press edition 2022

The Korean edition of this book was originally published by Munhakdongne
Publishing Group, Korea.

This book is published with the support of the Literature Translation Institute of
Korea (LTI Korea).

 This book was made possible thanks to a grant from the
New York State Council on the Arts with the support
of the Governor and the New York State Legislature.

 This book is supported in part by an award from the National
Endowment for the Arts.

Second printing September 2022

Cover design by Debbie Holmes, Orion Books
Cover photograph by Jeff Cottenden
Text design by Frances Ross

Library of Congress Cataloging-in-Publication Data
Names: Sin, Kyung-suk, author. | Hur, Anton, translator.
Title: Violets / Kyung-Sook Shin ; translated from the Korean by Anton Hur.
Other titles: Paiollet. English
Description: First Feminist Press edition. | New York City : The Feminist
    Press at the City University of New York, 2022.
Identifiers: LCCN 2021046098 (print) | LCCN 2021046099 (ebook) | ISBN
    9781558612907 (paperback) | ISBN 9781558612914 (ebook)
Subjects: LCGFT: Lesbian fiction.
Classification: LCC PL992.73.K94 P3513 2022 (print) | LCC PL992.73.K94
    (ebook) | DDC 895.73/4—dc23/eng/20211020
LC record available at https://lccn.loc.gov/2021046098
LC ebook record available at https://lccn.loc.gov/2021046099

PRINTED IN THE UNITED STATES OF AMERICA

Where the Minari Grows

A little girl.

One day in July, rain pours from the skies. In a house with shut doors, a mother closes her eyes as the baby's grandmother offers her the newborn. The mother knows what will happen now. An uncelebrated girl. The infant accepts her mother's closed eyes in lieu of a loving caress, perhaps having intuited her fate from the womb, and does not bother crying. The sound of the monsoon fills the house. Underneath the porch, a dog curls its legs into itself.

Can the baby hear the sound of the rain? She's about to fall asleep in her grandmother's hands. That same night, her father gives his daughter's face only a cursory glance.

The mother's postpartum depression lasts a long time. A swaddling blanket embroidered with faded roses has usurped her former dreams. The city life. High heels. Glass doors opening into restaurants. Elevators. Shining displays of perfume bottles and pearls, brightly colored clothing. Only in the final month of her pregnancy did the mother wearily pack up her hopes of moving to the city one day, and sat at the edge of the porch stitching roses into the blanket the baby would lie on.

The newborn indeed lies on it now, sucking her own hand. While the new mother secludes herself at home with her baby, the monsoon passes, and then typhoons. Eventually four o'clocks grow

firm petals along the base of the courtyard walls, and little chrysanthemums bloom and dot the scene with yellow. It's these autumn
flowers that finally rouse the mother back to the land of the living,
as if the blooms help rally her feelings.

Their village has long been dominated by people with the Yi
family name. The Yis own the farmland and forests surrounding
the village. Having lived there for a long time, they possess a powerful sense of entitlement. Everyone who lives in the central part of
the village is named Yi. They are each other's aunts and cousins,
at most twice removed. Outsiders who trickle in have to settle in a
spot about fifty meters from the main village. It all looks like one
village, but there is an unspoken yet significant divide between
the main and new villages. The new villagers live by the grace or
silence of the main villagers; even after they've lived there for years,
they're still considered outsiders. The new villagers are people who
didn't have anywhere else to go after the Korean War, or who had
tried and failed at business in town, or were undeniable vagabonds
in the first place.

This story may be better off untold. It begins when the baby's
mother first moves to the village as a newlywed. Most other villagers are tenant farmers working on the Yi family's land or servants
in their houses, but uniquely her husband works at a shoe factory
located about an hour away by bus. Throughout her childhood,
his daughter could never find out if her father was a manager or
a factory-floor worker. Her grandmother, whenever she was asked
about her son, would either answer that he owned a shoe factory
or that he worked in one. No one could get a straight answer as to
whether he was someone who hired factory workers or a worker
himself. In any case, he was clearly not involved in the village's
main source of income, that of working in the fields.

Maybe things have changed, but back then farmers didn't ride
around on motorcycles, wearing helmets. And while the villagers

may have long forgotten the baby's rough-spoken grandmother or the melancholy mother, they must remember her tall father and his rakish gaze. His motorcycle pierced the dawn's silence on his way to work. How could they ever forget that strange sound, that flashing light, racing like a wild animal through the darkness? The Yis despised the noise of the machine as it ripped through the main village, but there was no way they could prevent him from riding that motorcycle. He wasn't like the other new villagers, who could be ordered around. Nor was he one to care about what people thought about him, so anyone who might bring it up would be left embarrassed by their own indignation. Better to just bear the noise. If anything, his pomade and his leather gloves and jacket became something of a fad. And the villagers' interest in the family had as much to do with the man's wife as his motorcycle. She was a rare beauty, all the more so in this relatively isolated hamlet, although her delicate face and clear skin would've attracted stares in any region. Black hair that shone softly in the sunlight, and well-balanced features that drew a smile from anyone who happened to glance her way. She had a poignant, tragic quality, shared by all women whose face, neck, waist, and legs seem to flow in an unbroken line. Tragedy resided not only in her appearance but also her life; generation after generation, her ancestors had owned a thousand pyeong in apple orchards until her father had fallen into gambling and lost it all. Her family had been relegated to a rented room in the mountains, and she had to drop out of middle school just as soon as she'd started.

She had once aspired to teach at a girls' school. Instead, she grew into womanhood in that rented room. Her family's finances showed no signs of recovering despite all their frugality and saving. Her only way out was marriage. And surely her now-husband had not planned to neglect her from the beginning. Originally, he was so smitten with her that it wouldn't have mattered even if she'd been carrying another man's child. But when the little girl named San is born, San's father—for whatever reason—begins to distance himself from his wife.

Does this story seem unfamiliar or extraordinary? It shouldn't. For countless generations women have suffered and wasted away in strange rooms just like this baby's mother. Just as the flowers lighting up the courtyard begin to wilt, the father leaves on his motorcycle early one morning like always—except that this time he does not return for over nine years. And the singular sound of the motorcycle ceases to be heard in the village.

The bewildered, abandoned woman is left with only her child and the child's grandmother. With no land to farm, and in order to support her daughter and mother-in-law, the woman ventures into town and learns hairdressing. As a person whose appearance always drew attention, it somehow fits that she becomes someone with hands that reek of perm chemicals. With no money to set up a real shop, the child's mother carries curling irons, scissors, and large combs from house to house, perming, curling, and cutting hair cheap. Her unhappiness stems not so much from the work, from lugging her implements door to door, but rather from her contentious relationship with her mother-in-law. San grows up listening to the two of them arguing over their meals, at the well, in the kitchen, or on the porch, the ruckus familiar as a lullaby.

One day, the child leaves behind the sound of their fighting and sets out looking for her friend Namae. The two little girls amuse themselves easily; they sweep ants into the floor cracks and burn them, or knock down their neighbors' drying laundry from the line with a pole.

Along the dike on the southern edge of the village is a field of wild minari.

This lush expanse connects the village to the outside world. The field might predate the village, and is truly vast. In the spring, wild minari sprouts through the mud, making the village appear as if embraced by a grassy plain. In July and August, the minari explodes into sprays of white flowers, but until then, the green spring field serves as an invigorating symbol of renewal for the otherwise drab hamlet. When the minari thickens, people come from all over to harvest it. Even the occasional leech clinging to their calves can't break the villagers' good cheer while gathering up the bounty. On Buddha's Birthday, a nearby temple always sends someone to gather minari for the monks' food. Children always get a plate of it for their first birthday feast, the long stems served stir-fried to symbolize a long life.

San's mother shreds fresh minari to put into kimchi. One day, San comes home from school wet from rain and ends up with a fever, and her mother mashes up some minari and boils it into a bitter tea. The village women hear about this and start administering similar teas to their children for indigestion or headaches. Some evenings, the village women use lightly cooked minari stalks to wrap boiled beef slices, peppers, strips of egg yolk, and pine nuts. The children turn their heads away at the bitter taste, but the adults cherish the flavor, remembering it into their twilight years. The few who have left the village always return seeking the taste of that minari. Once the distinctly fragrant season has passed, the villagers, without being directed by anyone, sprinkle the field with compost and chicken droppings. San plods over to the minari field on days her mother and grandmother fight and Namae can't be found. Even when only a swamp is left, a little child sits alone atop the dike.

Going to school is a journey made on foot, four kilometers away over a hill, as the bus only comes twice a day. The children gather in front of the village warehouse every morning before setting off together. Before they can get to the hill, there's a bridge to cross and a path through an acacia forest to walk. The Yi children tear across the bridge and through the woods on their bikes. But the other country-mouse children treat the four-kilometer journey as a series of challenges: who can run up to the bridge first, who can pile up more clay at the swamp, who can pick the most pine cones in the forest. When they make it over the hill and the red brick of the school building comes into view, they race to the gate. On their way home, the children are silent only when skirting past the ornery geese that guard the stationery store. They play rock-paper-scissors to determine who will carry all their bags for the next kilometer. Namae loses; San takes half of Namae's load, which earns her a grateful smile. San smiles back. The other children, freed from their bags, run ahead of them, kicking up dirt. They want to get to the end of the first kilometer. Shrouded in the ensuing dust cloud, the girls bear their burdens like religious ascetics, their feet heavy on the ground.

A motorbike, with a young woman riding on the back, covers the two girls in dust as it speeds by. San waves the cloud away from her face as she stares longingly at the motorbike. It sprays the children who had gone on ahead as well, eventually disappearing except for its sound. San finds it hard to tear her gaze away. She thinks of her grandmother. The ornery old woman pined for the sound of the motorcycle. She'd come running out of the house whenever she heard one go by, even midfight with San's mother. He may never come back for you, but he'll come back for me, she would say as she wet her parched lips and aged right before their eyes.

With the bags hoisted on her back, Namae walks down toward the irrigation ditch. Namae is as cheerful as you please. Namae's father, when drunk, would crawl into one of the large earthen jars arranged along their garden wall and sing. Nobody knew why he had to sing inside a jar. The singing would echo so much in that confined space that it was impossible to make out any words. His failed attempts at words would mush together. The singing would continue until he exhausted himself and fell asleep. Namae would then crouch down by the garden gate or at the end of their porch and sob, wringing her hands. But the Namae walking down to the ditch now, carrying three bags on her back, is not that sobbing Namae. Namae is not a Yi but a Sur. Just as San is not Yi San but Oh San. They are not like the Yi children, who already feel entitled thanks to their name. And because San is without a father, the Yi children's stares are especially superior. If they happen to be playing together and their fathers walk by, they shout "Daddy!" and abandon San and cling to their fathers with extra enthusiasm. They call each other by their given names, Sa-ok or Gwi-soon, but they never forget to discriminate by using her full name, Oh San. Namae, also not a Yi, gets called Sur Namae. Perhaps it was inevitable that Oh San and Sur Namae would fall into intimacy, calling each other San and Namae when the other children were not around. Namae's father, when he isn't drunk, is a gentle soul who indulges his daughter. Every morning before she goes to school, he brushes her long hair, braids her ponytail, and sweeps the braid over her shoulder to the front. Namae never mentions this side of her father to San. And San never mentions her mother to Namae. Just as San has heard Namae's father singing in the jar, Namae has seen San's mother and grandmother argue. The fact they each have something to be ashamed of makes the two draw closer. They are two stragglers from the herd. It makes Namae sad to see her drunk father climb into the jar to cry. Namae says her mother probably died because she couldn't bear his crying. That she herself will someday die because of her father.

"Why does your father crawl into the jar to sing?"

"He says he can't hear anything otherwise, even when he's listening carefully."

"Even when he's listening carefully?"

"Even when he's listening carefully!"

Once Namae's father is exhausted from singing, he falls asleep in the jar. On such nights, young Namae brings out a blanket, covers her father with it, and goes to sleep outside leaning against the jar, ear pressed against its glazed surface. Even when San stands right next to Namae, Namae doesn't say anything or tell her to go away. Two nothing-girls. They've learned how to console each other without saying a word. Little San sleeps next to Namae, who has her ear against the jar, with her own ear against Namae.

Namae lugs the three bags past the dike and into a graveyard overgrown with weeds. She seems to have an idea and gestures at San. San hesitates, looking at the receding children, and goes down to the dike. Namae has placed the bags on a grassy burial mound and is lying on her stomach on top of it. San can see the village in the distance. They have so much farther to go. She approaches, and Namae grabs her hand.

"Listen carefully."

The two girls lie on the mound, their ears pressed against its gentle curve. The smell of earth and grass is sharp in their noses.

"This is my mother's grave. She's our guardian angel from now on. She's watching over us wherever we go."

A day in May.

Her mother's hand grips a pair of scissors. Like some windup toy, her grandmother repeats herself over and over again: Her son left and won't come back because his wife was frigid. The scissors are a chilling sight. Unable to bear the suspense, San thrusts her feet into her shoes and runs out the garden gate. The paved road sprawls pitifully under the sun. A dog with a low-hanging tail saunters by. Slate roofs, some red, some blue, lie flat in the background. Trees peek out through the open gates of the other houses. Unruly patches of weeds overgrow onto the main road. The branches of the persimmon tree next door stretch over the wall, brilliantly laden with white flowers. The girl called San is overcome with a compulsion to smash and shatter against something. She leans against the wall that the persimmon tree reaches over. She rubs her face against it. Her forehead becomes scratched and beads with blood. Afraid, San breaks into a run. The blood from her forehead flows down her cheeks. She wants to get as far away as possible. Even better, she thinks, if she never has to come back.

The minari field is green. Summer is coming. San is drenched with sweat as she runs, her sweat mingled with blood. She goes down to the irrigation ditch and washes her face, splashing palmfuls of water. Her forehead throbs. She climbs to the top of the dike, from where she can see the whole field, and plops down. She almost writhes with the sudden, agonizing loneliness. There is no one picking minari today. Is it because of the prickly sunlight? A sad blue sky floats over the road and the minari. She puts a hand to her forehead and checks to see if blood smears off on her palm. It doesn't, but the scratched spot still throbs, and she blinks away the sweat in her eyes. She lies down and puts her ear against the dike and looks down on the whole field where the minari grows. What could she hear if she listened hard enough? Could she hear the thoughts of her father, who left as soon as she was born; the feelings of her grandmother, who ripped into her mother time and again; the rage of her mother, who gripped the flashing shears in her hand? As she blinks, the green seeps into her mind like a bitter taste. She shuts her eyes. Her wound throbs and throbs in the sun.

She opens her eyes because her face tickles. Namae squats before her, wearing a white shirt and blue shorts, holding a blade of foxtail. The bushy part pokes San's face. Namae's braided ponytail is neatly settled on her shirt front. Their eyes meet, Namae's eyes brimming with mirth, San's drowning in sadness. Namae looks into San's eyes for a moment before gently cupping San's face.

"What happened?"

San is silent.

"Did you trip?"

Little San is too afraid to reply. How could she describe the heat she felt when she put her forehead to the wall? The desire to crash into something. A desire she still feels in her heart. Instead of responding, she grabs the foxtail from Namae's hand and pushes it up Namae's nose. Jerking her head back in surprise, Namae loses her balance and rolls down the dike. There's a splash, and the stirred-up silt turns the stream muddy and opaque. Namae gets up, her eyes and nose red from swallowing water. San is caught off guard when Namae reaches up and pulls her in. Upon contact, the cold water fires up the wound on her forehead. One of her shoes comes off, and Namae races to save it. Placing their shoes on top of the dike, the two girls start splashing each other. The waterweeds are dancing. The two keep slipping as they play, and soon their lips are as blue as ink. San's wound, which she had briefly forgotten about, aches with a pain that stretches to her nose. The two scramble up the dike, take a look at each other, and giggle, water dripping down their clothes and hair. They shake their heads to get the water off. The flying droplets hit each other's faces. Namae hesitates as she looks down at her soaked clothes. She takes off her blue shorts, squeezes them dry, and spreads them on the dike. San follows suit, taking off her raindrop-print skirt, squeezing it, and also laying it out in the sun. Namae's white shirt and San's yellow blouse are next. Then, with some reluctance, Namae takes off her underwear, shakes out the water, and lays it out as well. San takes off her own underwear, squeezes it, shakes it, and lays it out. Both naked, they stretch out side by side like a pair of chopsticks. Now that their wet clothes are off, sunlight returns warmth to their bodies. Little San thinks the dike must be a green mirror; Namae's bare body looks identical to her own. If she reaches out to the pink forehead in her reflection, it will ache just like hers. The black pupils of her eyes, the braid falling down her little shoulder, the small cheeks where the water has already dried, the narrow bridge of her nose. San feels reassured that Namae's body is as skinny and pathetic as her own.

"Look there," says Namae, pointing to the sky. "It's watching us."

Namae giggles as she props herself up. The move reveals her back, and San stares, dazzled. There is a green grass stain blotting Namae's small, sloped back; the blot is softly, tenderly spread across the white. Without thinking about it, San reaches out with her fingers to touch the spot when Namae whips around.

Their eyes meet.

"You saw it!"

San is speechless.

"You saw the birthmark on my back, right?" Namae's voice trembles. "I didn't want anyone to see it."

San says nothing.

"I'd forgotten about it." Namae's eyes fill with tears of rage. "What is it anyway, a Mongolian spot?"

But San smiles brightly. So this must be why San has never seen Namae playing in the stream with the others.

"I . . . thought it was a grass stain."

"Are you making fun of me?"

"It's really pretty. Turn around. I want to see it."

"No."

Namae sticks out her tongue in pointed refusal and promptly lies down on her back. Their bodies feel downy as they dry. Namae had acted as if she would never again show San her spot, lying down with her back flat against the grass, but she soon shifts her position and rolls onto her side. San follows suit. The green-blue spot that is not a grass stain flashes in San's vision. How beautiful it is.

"You have something I don't have."

Little San begins to feel sad. This blot, only found on Namae's back, threatens their being two of a kind. The girls prop their heads up on their palms and stare out over the field, eyes filled with the vast stretch of minari. The green undulates. How could the world be so quiet? The road is empty, the irrigation ditch is empty, and the field is empty. Where has everyone gone?

The girls are lying on their stomachs, waving their feet in the air, when their anklebones painfully collide. Namae, still prone, pulls in her anklebone and rubs it. San sits up in pain and rubs her own anklebone. She looks down at Namae's curled body. The green blot on her white back is arched and clear. San's hand slowly reaches out and touches the soft outline of the green blot, following it with her fingers. Namae flinches but lies still, not breathing. In this unexpected silence, little San cannot fight off the melancholy that crashes into her. It travels over the minari field in waves.

"You have something no one else has."

Namae releases her foot, and caresses San's forehead instead.

"Does it hurt a lot?"

San doesn't respond.

"Why did you do this?"

Namae blows soothingly on San's wound. The urge inside to collide into something, that uncontrollable impulse San thought she'd managed to tamp down, is welling up again. The hand that traced the blot on Namae's pale back begins to rub Namae's neck. A passing breeze ruffles the grass on the dike. The minari bends in the wind. San is about to cry when Namae pulls her into an embrace. When their warm bodies meet, San feels a surge of loneliness she's sure will last for the rest of her life. Their soft lips touch, and their little fingers tangle together for a moment. Namae sits bolt upright and swats San's back, but San pulls her down again. They awkwardly fall into an embrace, look into each other's eyes, and settle down on the grass once more.

The next time San opens her eyes, it's to the quacking of some passing ducks. She's alone on the dike. White ducks with yellow beaks play in the ditch where Namae had fallen earlier. San stares at the blank spaces between her raindrop-print skirt, her yellow blouse, and her white underwear. The spaces where Namae's white shirt, blue shorts, and underwear had been.

Little San puts on her clothes and sits, staring out at the minari. Why did Namae leave without her? Suddenly, San is afraid. There's not a single cloud in the sky. Waves of green swell. The silence is eerie. A red cloud of dust rises from the road and melts into the field. San sits there until the sound of the ducks fade and twilight descends. A villager who has come to pick minari sees her sitting stock-still and calls out her name, but San doesn't reply. She may not have heard. Eventually, San gets up, despite her wounded forehead and aching ankle, and gets off the dike. She heads for Namae's house. The house has its lights on, but is quiet. Only Namae's shoes greet her from beneath the porch. By the wall, next to the well, is the large earthen jar that Namae's father crawls into, its mouth gaping in the dusk. San can't bring herself to call Namae's name. She simply stands there. Namae refuses to come out. Little San drags her feet to the jar and crawls inside. The floor and walls are icy to the touch. She crouches and listens carefully. But there's only the cold. There's only darkness. Overcome with dread, she lets out an *Ah—*. Her voice is small, but it rings within the jar. *Ahhh—*. Surprised by her own voice, she clamps her mouth and stops breathing. There's the sound of an opening door, and the sound of Namae putting on her shoes. San squeezes her eyes shut in the already black interior. Come, my love. Come and raise me from this darkness. Little San listens carefully to each of Namae's approaching footsteps.

Namae's shadow covers the mouth of the jar.

"Get out!" Namae shouts. San is crouched, her eyes squeezed shut.

San doesn't move.

"I said, get out!"

Finally, little San crawls out of the jar.

Namae pushes her and yells, "Go away!" Namae rushes to her house, takes off her shoes, and darts back inside where a faint glow seeps out. But where is San supposed to go? To whom? A thought sweeps across her heart: If she leaves now, she'll never see Namae again. That must never happen.

Have you forgotten me? Already?

How warm we were by the minari. The beautiful green blot staining your white back. The gentleness of your cheek. Your small hand that caressed the wound on my forehead.

The jar stands and stares with listless shoulders. A few moments later, Namae opens the door and looks out into the yard. She sees San standing there and screams at her to leave. When San doesn't move, she runs out of the house and thumps her on the chest with a fist.

"All right," says Namae abruptly, and walks away.

San tries to say something as she follows Namae to the kitchen. Namae, surprised by San trailing her, leaves through a door to the backyard. The more San thinks she should say something, the more her lips freeze.

Namae comes back into the kitchen, biting her lower lip, and grabs the knife sitting on the chopping board as she orders San outside. Namae runs to the chicken coop on the other side of the yard. She throws open the coop door and grabs one of the birds by the wings, a red cock, and pulls it out. She is holding the screaming rooster with one hand and with the other she thrusts the knife at San. Not knowing what to do, San takes it from her.

"Now, follow me."

Namae leads San to the large stone mortar next to the well and glares at her.

"Cut off its head."

San doesn't move.

"I said, cut off the head of this cock!"

She still doesn't move.

"You can't?"

". . ."

"Then get out!"

". . ."

"I said, get out!"

San feels like the backyard walls are closing in. Dizzy, she almost drops the knife. The white back hidden inside your white shirt, the luscious green blot spread across that back. Your soft lips, your warm body. Little San had not anticipated this situation back when she was tracing Namae's spot with her fingers. She doesn't know how to take in what's happening. She feels numb. Your warm body, the ribs that protruded over the pit of your stomach, your delicately rising and falling uvula—where has this betrayal been hiding? But if it means I can be with you, San thinks. If it means you won't leave me. She closes her eyes. She raises the knife. I can't go back like this! She thrusts the knife into the rooster's neck and pulls.

Silence.

Their vision clouds over. The head of the rooster is rolling on the ground. There are droplets of blood splattered on the well. Namae, in shock, rolls on the ground and clutches the rooster still squirming with life. San drops the knife, and Namae tosses aside the headless cock. Red blood covers the earthen jar, the wall, the well, and the two girls. Namae stumbles away from San, then screams at her as she scrambles onto the porch with her shoes still on and falls inside the house. She locks the door shut behind her.

San's mother ends up throwing the shears at San's grandmother.

Her grandmother's forehead is injured, and this incident forces San's father to finally return to the village. Riding a car, not a motor-cycle. With two new children and a new wife. Despite her years of sacrifice, San's mother is deemed irredeemable for throwing scissors at her own mother-in-law. Lifelessly and without protest, she signs the divorce papers. This makes San's mother the first divorced woman in the village. The family has split; now San is only her mother's daughter. The father and grandmother promptly banish the mother and daughter, sell the house, and move to another village with their new family. Whenever San feels overwhelmed by each new development, she seeks out Namae's company, but she is spurned every time. Even when San visits on nights where Namae's father is singing inside the jar, Namae throws rocks at her. She screams not to come any closer. When they had put their sun-dried clothes back on, the two girls' feelings had completely diverged. Little San had felt, I will love you more than myself. Namae had felt, This is the end of the oath we made on the grave. She had said goodbye to San forever.

San and her mother end up renting a room in a big house in the village. From time to time, San's mother bursts into laughter at nothing in particular. San herself almost never ventures anywhere beyond home and school until the day they leave the village for good. At most, someone might occasionally catch a glimpse of her listening to a grave on her way home, or staring at the hens and ducks in the yard of the big house, or sitting alone for hours on the dike that overlooks where the minari grows.

A Woman to Look After Flowers

The flower shop in the early summer is verdant and radiant.

The windows, even the outer shutters, are opened to the street. The sidewalk in front of the shop is wet, as if someone has just sprinkled a hose there. Pots of ficus trees, rubber figs, and lady palms populate the sidewalk. When annoyed pedestrians walk by, their frowns melt into contented sighs at the sight of lush green plants, purple balloon flowers, and buckets filled with China pinks and irises.

This flower shop is an unexpected oasis. It faces the parking lot of Seoul's Sejong Center for the Performing Arts, acting as a brief respite from the busy noise of surrounding traffic.

A conveyor-belt sushi restaurant serving twin pieces of sushi or egg rolls on each plate, a Paris Baguette bakery franchise, a kimbap place barely squeezing in three tables, a stone-bowl rice shop, a 24-hour convenience store, a foreign language cram school, a stationery shop, a store specializing in photo albums, a bookstore kiosk set up between buildings, a new Mediterranean-style pasta place, a café named Spring Summer Autumn Winter—and amid all these stores is a flower shop of considerable size, looking somewhat out of place, almost cinematic.

Wanted: A woman to look after flowers.

San has returned to this flower shop. She walked away from it two days ago. She sighs in relief when she sees the white paper sign still up on the glass door. The sun shines on the building, the gleaming asphalt, and the brass knocker on a nearby wooden door. Soon enough, this freshness of early summer will give way to real heat: humidity, the sun beating down, people afraid of their sandals melting into the pavement.

San discovered the flower shop two days ago, when she spotted it from inside a phone booth by the Sejong Arts Center across the street. San had just gotten off the phone with the publishing house she'd interviewed with ten days earlier. Their newspaper ad had caught her eye after she'd been demoralized by the many rejections from agencies that her cram school had sent her on interviews to. Despite the publisher's promise to contact her soon, there had been no news for those ten days. After much deliberation, she had finally called them. Her expectations had been low, because during her interview they had seemed disappointed by her lack of professional experience. All the same, upon hearing that the new word processor operator had already started four days ago, she sagged against the wall of the phone booth.

She had really wanted to work at that publishing house.

Because it was near a subway station, and hanging on the door were photographs of writers she admired. Because if she'd been hired, she would have met those writers and worked with them on their manuscripts. But perhaps what had really attracted her to this elusive publisher was the fact that the office was not in a glass tower but in a house with a yard. The publisher was in a residential area.

New buildings were being built along the main road nearby, but the company was in an older, two-story Western-style house. The house rested comfortably between two new buildings. Her interview had looked down at a magnolia tree in a yard with a wide-open gate. The tree was so big that it was plainly visible from the other side of the wall. There was a parasol beneath it, under which employees had gathered for a coffee break. Surely there must have been a flock of white blossoms in the spring, but the tree had now replaced them with green leaves. It grazed the sky and the new surrounding buildings.

San regrets not mentioning that, despite her lack of experience, she could accurately type up to five hundred characters per minute. That had been another reason to feel excited about working at this particular publisher. The word processing textbooks at her cram school had been so boring that she moved on to practicing with novels and essays. She had typed out an essay collection called *Memories of an Old Shirt* so many times she could practically recite the book. The author was one of the writers adorning the publisher's front door. After her interview, she took one last look at the parasol beneath the magnolia. She hoped that she, too, would sit there and drink coffee someday.

While she waited, she had tried to keep up her spirits as much as possible. Every morning when she opened her eyes and heard the birds chirping in the grounds of the Prime Minister's office, she took it as a sign that the publisher would call her. The mountain spring at Samcheong Park was so full that it was easy to scoop up clear water, and she saw this as a good omen. Even when ten days passed without any word, she still thought she might get the job. But wilting inside the phone booth, lost in disappointment, her eyes had fallen on this flower shop.

She had left the booth and crossed the street as if the shop was calling to her. The harsh sun ambushed her, pricking her eyes as soon as she left the shade, but no matter. Only when she came to a stop, standing by the summer flowers in their blue buckets and the green trees taking up half the sidewalk, did she feel light-headed from the sudden heat.

A woman to look after flowers.

Through her dizziness, she read the neatly written words. That morning, she had put her hair up with an unadorned, chestnut-colored hairpin, pinning it above the downy and delicate nape of her neck. She put on a watery blue dress. Two days ago, when she had first come across this advertisement for a female florist, San had abruptly turned as if shocked. Someone would've thought she had a very pressing matter to attend to, or that she was being pursued. That was how quick her steps were.

Then, her swift and silent legs stopped in their tracks. She brought a hand to her forehead as if to ward off the heat and she took a moment to catch her breath. The air, already laden with summer, enveloped her. Standing there she thought, But I must work. She could still hear the matter-of-fact voice of the person on the phone, informing her that the new hire had already started.

Two days earlier, San had turned and walked back to the flower shop. She walked slowly, unlike how she had fled just a moment ago. She went back and looked down at the blue bucket by the glass door. It was filled with white buds, round and waiting to burst, and there was a slightly smaller bucket beside it, filled with bouquets of red roses and baby's breath. Inside the flower shop was a middle-aged man, all alone, wiping dust off the leaves of a sago palm.

Her goal had been to become a word processor operator. When she gave up working as a hairdresser's assistant after two years, everyone said she was a fool. Why would she spend money on computer courses when she was almost good enough to be a hairstylist on her own? But the truth was she couldn't bear to spend her days in a salon any longer.

It was two years of having bits of other people's hairs stuck on her everywhere, underneath her ears, her fingernails, in her armpits. When she came home late at night, she took off her work clothes, showered to within an inch of her life, and prepared to lie down — when a bit of clinging hair would fall on the bedding. One time, a prick in her eye made her get up in the middle of the night, and it turned out to be a fragment of hair on her pupil. Her eyes had suffered from phantom stings ever since, a constant irritation; she imagined particles of hair piercing her eyeballs.

When she'd quit the salon and enrolled in cram school to learn how to use a Mac, she hadn't set out to become a word processor operator. She had also embarked on a graphic design course, but eventually had to concede her lack of talent. Someone else in her cohort went on to a high-salaried job at an animation company, but the only work San could do with any competence was editing documents and typing. She was so immersed in the latter that her resting hands would tap on any surface as if it were a keyboard. Waiting for a bus, her ten fingers would neatly type on a nearby tree, *I am waiting for a bus*. But despite her efforts, she failed every test and interview for word processing.

Two days ago, as she stood in her blue dress with her hair done up with a plain pin, her eyes had met those of the middle-aged man looking up from the sago palm. Instead of walking through the crowded blue buckets and entering the shop, she avoided his gaze and walked away. She thought, This shop sits right on the street. If I get a job here, I'd have to be here all day, and I don't want to feel like I'm peddling wares like a street vendor.

And yet, here she stands before the flower shop again.

Her landlady woke her up that morning. San lives in a long second-floor apartment that looks down onto a street lined with ginkgo trees. Outside her window she can see a café, a high wall, and a rice merchant a bit farther out. On the ground floor, below her oddly long room, is a realtor's office with rattan chairs. She got the room from an old man who dozed in one of those tattered, scratched chairs. Next to the realtor's door is another door leading to a narrow corridor lined with shelves, upon which small folding tables are stacked. The tables too big to be shelved are pushed against the corridor wall. Walking through the corridor leads into the inner annex. The landlady's family and their three daughters, each a year apart in age, live in these rooms. Beside the entrance to these rooms is a flight of nine stairs going up to the second floor. The bathroom is at the bottom of the stairs. At the top of the stairs are two doors, and the one on the right is the door to San's long room. The door on the left has a sign saying "Recreation Office." The street-facing window has a sign saying the same thing. Recreation Office. San has never seen the door open. She only reads the sign as she comes and goes.

San recalls how, still groggy, she heard the landlady's footsteps making their way up the stairs that morning. The landlady called out, *Miss*, with every step she took, presumably wanting San to come out before she had to reach the top, but San hadn't even risen yet. Only when the landlady was on the seventh stair did San open her door, the collar of her thrown-on shirt still folded into the neckline.

The landlady with three daughters had her hair pinned up and wore a smile. She looked young for forty. She must've been reading the news before coming up, because she held a newspaper in her hand. The landlady sat down on a stair instead of coming up and entering the room, so San stood in the doorway, looking down at her.

The landlady was there to inform San she was raising the rent. *I regret to inform you*, she added in an apologetic tone. And she didn't forget to add that the room was still cheaper than most other places. Cheaper? It would've been fine for an office or a store, but the room's windows opened onto the street, making it too noisy to sleep or eat or even think properly. The road outside her window is the only way for cars coming out of Samcheong Tunnel to get to Gwanghwamun Gate, Sajik Tunnel, or Anguk-dong, making the noise inevitable. Thankfully, the building shares a wall with the Prime Minister's office, which means security is always tight. It was the first thing the landlady had pointed out about the room, that San needn't bother locking her door at night. No one in this neighborhood does, she said. But San always locks her door. As long as she has a window that opens onto the street, she can never let her guard down like the Prime Minister, even if she shares a wall with his office.

The landlady wanted to increase the key money by two million won. To buy a piano. Her eldest daughter loves to play, she explained, but because she didn't have her own piano at home, she apparently had taken to wandering around searching for one to practice on.

"All she does after school is drop off her bag and go looking for a piano."

"Where does she go?"

"To the Catholic church or wherever."

A child in search of a piano.

The landlady's expression and tone were sincerely sympathetic. "We were saving money and only have a little bit more to go, but something strange is happening. Our daughter is being bullied for looking around for a piano. If she stays behind at her piano lessons to practice, the other children make fun of her for showing off. They call her weird for wanting to learn piano when she doesn't even have a piano at home. Some kid slapped her, too."

" . . . "

"She won't tell me who it was. Something about getting bullied more if she told. I just can't bear it as a mother to see her moping around with her head down."

San thought of her savings. She didn't have much left. Almost all the money she had put away during her two years at the salon had been spent on computer classes. The installment savings account she had begun with the hopes of buying a nice big wooden table had been neglected for months now. The landlady went on about how sales were bad on top of everything else. The landlady's family sold foldable tables; San had bought a little tea table herself. She stared at a black butterfly clinging to the inside of her screen window and said, *All right.* When the landlady went back down the narrow staircase, San picked up the newspaper she had left behind.

Motorcycle kidnappings on the rise. Motorcycle gangs infiltrate residential areas. Around 9 p.m. last night, Miss Hong (anon), a word processor operator coming home from work, was kidnapped not fifty meters away from her home, taken to a playground, and assaulted. She was discovered much later and died on her way to the hospital.

San stared at the words *Miss Hong (anon), a word processor operator* for a long time before carefully taking the black butterfly's wings between her fingers. Only the backdrop of its wings was black; they were otherwise dotted with yellow and white. Insects flew into or clung to the window at every opportunity. She brought the butterfly on to her palm and tried to get it to fly but it just sat, not going anywhere. Before leaving for the bathhouse, she placed the exhausted creature on the top of her minifridge and decided to drop by the flower shop. She would see if they were still hiring, and if so, work there until she found a word processing job.

Now, back in front of the flower shop, she takes several deep breaths.

The middle-aged man from before, who had been wiping the palm leaves, is watering a row of orchids displayed side by side in lush splendor. Unlike the previous time when she had hesitated, San looks directly at his back as she walks into the shop.

It's larger than it looks from the outside. As she enters, she's assaulted by the smell of plants. Flowers hang from pots, so pretty that her heart aches. Some trees reach the ceiling and others seem to have just been unearthed, their roots and soil balled up in plastic.

At her entrance, the man watering orchids turns around. He looks at her for a moment as she stands among the trees. Somehow, he seems to know that she's not there to buy flowers or a tree. Putting down his can, he walks toward her, framed by the orchids. He takes a chair out from under an old metal drafting table covered in white paper, colorful ribbons, and sashes used for wrapping bouquets, and places it before her. He wipes the water-splattered chair with a towel. Then, he takes out a notepad from his shirt pocket and writes something before handing it to her. A pen dangles on the notepad.

Please sit.

A man who speaks through a notepad.

San reads the words and sits down.

The man writes some more.

I knew you would come back.

San says nothing as she stares at this man who does not speak but writes down words for her to read. The man, evidently used to such stares, doesn't look fazed.

He writes again. *You were here a few days ago but you left.*

"Yes."

Why did you flee?

San smiles at the sentence held out to her. His handwriting is jagged, but the precise straightness of his lines makes it look neat.

He writes, *Have you ever worked at a flower shop?*

It was the same kind of question she'd been asked in her interviews.

Feeling awkward speaking aloud to a man who writes, San writes instead, next to his words, *I never have.* The man's tall handwriting contrasts with her rounded style.

The man seems disappointed as he looks her up and down and writes, *The work here is harder than it looks.*

He pauses.

Quite a few people have underestimated how hard it would be and quit after a few days.

San writes, *It ought to be easier than a hair salon.*

You worked at a hair salon?

Yes.

Not wanting to seem indecisive, she firmly dots the period after her *Yes.* She has a premonition that if she fails to get this job, she will fail to get any job ever again. She still nurses a twinge of unease, feeling a little like she's only one step above a street vendor. And the unease of wasting six months of computer classes is palpable. But there's also the thought that a flower shop would be preferable to the stench of perm chemicals, the metallic snipping of scissors, and the hot blasts of hairdryers.

I'll work very hard, she writes, putting strength into her wrist.

How much would you like to be paid?

She sits for a moment, the pen in her hand.

How much did they pay you at the salon?

She puts the pen down and says in a low voice, "Eight hundred thousand won a month."

Nervous, her eyes turn from the written conversation they're having to a white car slipping into the parking lot across the street.

Su-ae will show you the ropes when she comes back from vacation.

Su-ae?

She understands the work here even better than I do. I hope you two get along. After a pause, he asks, *What is your name?*

Oh San, she writes.

As if committing it to memory, the man studies her name for a long time. San takes this as an opportunity to give the flower shop owner a quick once-over. Small stature, hollow cheeks, a broad forehead. Perhaps sensing that she's looking at him, the flower shop man smiles and begins writing again.

I can't speak. But I can hear. So you can talk.

Shot through with giddiness, she tries to sit still.

There's a farm in Gupabal. Lots of trees. If you work here, you have to go there once in a while and help me with the work. Pot the trees, spread the fertilizer, make the plants grow in the pots as well as they do in the ground. Do you think you can do this?

She nods vigorously.

Trees are like people. They grow well if you love and care for them, and wither if you don't. I tried it out myself. It was true! I gave the same amount of nutrients to the same trees, but I looked at one group more and talked to them more and petted them more. The roots of the other group turned yellow in comparison.

The flower shop owner stops writing. He stands up and takes an emerald hose and affixes it to a tap. He turns the tap on and clear water promptly flows from the hose.

He comes back to the table and writes again. *I'd like you to start immediately. Is that possible?*

She nods.

You can begin by mopping the floor.

San hoses down the floor of the flower shop. Pots of sago palms, ficus trees, and rubber figs crowd the narrow passageways. The gloom from this morning washes away along with the earth on the floor. The flower shop owner indicates that he has a lunch appointment, washes his hands, and puts on his coat. He writes that if it weren't for her, he would've had to close the flower shop to keep his appointment. He tells her she ought to order lunch from one of the restaurants around the shop and leaves her a ₩10,000 note next to the twine on the table.

San is now a florist at a shop looking out onto the street.

Though it has only just happened, it seems like she's worked there for years. She turns the tap and the water ceases. She hesitates over where to put the watering can the man used, so she finds a toolbox, hammers a nail to the back of a display case, and hangs the can on the nail. Her hands straighten and organize the scattered sheets of paper and the multicolored ribbons. Her movements—gathering water and sprinkling it on the sidewalk outside the shop, washing rags and wiping dust off the windowsills and displays—illustrate how much the work revitalizes her. She handles the stems of the purple prairie gentians with such love and care that time settles into a fixed point, a single moment when her soul feels finally realized.

Since San had originally wanted to work at a publishing house, happiness doesn't quite feel like the right word. But her bustling makes her seem content. Her cheeks are flushed and soon they shimmer. Moving about, she discovers new seedlings or a bush she's never seen before, and her lips part and her pupils shine in quiet amazement. Whenever she reaches up to wipe the sweat off her brow, her waist peeks out shyly from underneath her shirt.

After a little while, she rests her elbow on the table, looking out onto the street.

The phone booth from where she called the publishing house comes directly into view. The vacant booth lazily returns her stare. A young woman walks by, talking on her cell phone. San tears her gaze away and looks back and forth between the road and the sidewalk. A high schooler with dyed blond hair rollerblades past, carrying a plastic bag that reads "Paris Baguette." San observes a white car drive into the lot and park beneath a tree. The rear window sticker proclaims "Beginner Driver." The fountain behind the Sejong Arts Center sprays cool jets of water into the sky. People are gathered at the fountain. Someone plays the guitar, singing a story about a girl who carves her name into a tree . . . the tree dropping a flower . . . the tree being heartbroken over the girl . . . the tree begging her to tell him what has become of his flower . . . San's eyes travel back to where they started. Her propped elbow looks as lonely as the empty phone booth.

She looks around the shop.

It's clear her earlier contentment, when she bustled about sprinkling water and handling flowers and hammering nails, has faded. A hollow silence forms inside the summer afternoon, in that variegated cocoon of flowers and trees. The sounds of real life — the laughter of young women walking into Sapporo Udon House and the car driving off into the street — move further away from her. Somewhere, on a faraway beach she's never been to, pebbles are soaking in this same summer sunlight. Somewhere there's a mountain path she's never stepped on, a seam of packed clay enduring a windless silence. Somewhere, someone she doesn't know wishes for meaningful conversation, biting her little finger in loneliness. Her elbow slips. Just as she rubs the ache, a man in a neat gray suit strides into the shop. He's inside before she can even stand up from her chair.

"Where's Su-ae?"

Su-ae?

San remembers the name from the owner's notepad. The Su-ae who knows how to run the shop better than the florist himself.

"She's on vacation."

"And who are you, miss?"

Who am I?

She is briefly at a loss as to how to introduce herself.

The man's gaze bores into her.

"I started working here today."

"I see. Miss Choi must've quit?"

Miss Choi? Now who was that?

"I need to send a pot from our company to an event in Samseong-dong. What am I supposed to do?"

"The owner will come back after lunch. If you tell me what you need, I'll let him know."

"Would you? Give me a piece of paper. I'll write down what the sash needs to say. We want a tall banyan tree, and tell him we want the letters nice and large. It should be eye-catching."

She finds some notepaper sticking out of a bookshelf but hovers about in search of a pen. The man, taking the paper from her, says he already has a pen. He bends over as he writes something down and from that position tosses a line to San, standing there with her fingers knotted together.

"I'm Choi Hyun-li."

Surprised at the man's unexpected introduction, she takes a step back.

Did he find her reaction unusual? The man, Choi Hyun-li, stops writing and looks up at her. Despite her shrinking back in suspicion, he laughs. Feeling awkward, she steps back farther in silence until he puts pen to paper again on the desk.

He adds, "Now you're making me feel bad . . . I only told you my name because you have a nice smile. We'll see each other again often enough."

Only then does she take a close look at him.

He is so tall that he has to bend almost perpendicularly to write on the table. Hair buzzed short, like an athlete. A clear razor line where his hair meets the back of his neck. Black shoes that shine, as if they'd been cleaned right before coming to the flower shop.

A white ramie shirt underneath the gray jacket. A blunt nose, a neat mouth, little wrinkles by his eyes when he smiles. He's the kind of person that gives off a good impression, which makes San think she herself must be strange by reacting this way. At least Choi doesn't seem offended by her defensiveness. Is it because of his height and the wrinkles when he smiles, or the ramie shirt? Despite wearing a suit on a summer day, he still looks cool and crisp.

"What a pretty young lady." He's still bent over as he writes, but he's talking as if he's been staring at her this whole time. "The plant should be at the event by 3:00 p.m. tomorrow, so I'll call in the morning to confirm."

Choi gives her shoulder a playful tap.

She retreats like before, unaware that she's even doing so. Her face turns red. Choi grins, looking amused. He seems to think she's cute.

"Don't let me down."

He gives her a slight wave and heads out.

A little dazed, she watches him walk toward the Sejong Arts Center fountain until she loses sight of him in the crowd and among all the fluttering banners announcing a rock concert. Languid sunshine pools on the asphalt where he's disappeared. The glare from the street hurts her eyes and she looks away. Recalling his touch, she brushes off the place where Choi tapped her shoulder. It feels like a gust of wind has come and gone, instead of Choi Hyun-li, and that wind has fluttered her skirt. Feeling inexplicably insulted, she stands and stares at Choi's handwriting on the note.

Two hours later, the flower shop owner comes back.

She hasn't had lunch, but nods when the owner asks her if she has. Is it because she's still tense? All she had that morning was some black tea with milk, but she's still not hungry. The man sees the ₩10,000 note but doesn't ask about it.

The weather is good all afternoon.

As if he's forgotten he hired her that morning, the shop owner gives San no further instructions but continues to sell flowers, trims trees, and writes up a sash according to Choi's note. Someone must've been appointed to a high position. The message says simply, *Congratulations to Chairperson Yi Sangcheol on his appointment.* The flower shop owner writes the black words on the blue sash as if he's done it many times before. When he realizes she's watching, he grins and writes, *How's your calligraphy?*

"Awful." Her cheeks redden.

The man looks a bit worried, writing, *Su-ae hates writing. But we need at least one of you to do it.* He thinks for a bit more before adding, *Do you know how to use a computer?*

Next to this she writes, *A little.*

Su-ae . . . San wonders what this young woman on vacation looks like. She's never met Su-ae but, having heard her name a few times, she begins to feel familiar. It'll be fine as long as Su-ae isn't like Miss Jung from the Segeumjeong salon. Unlike San, Miss Jung had graduated from beauty school and hated the fact that their salary was similar despite San's lack of credentials. Miss Jung complained whenever she had to do things like wash hair, apply chemicals, sweep the floors, launder the towels, or wipe the mirrors, always saying she was ready to cut hair *now.* She "accidentally" stepped on San's feet and smeared rancid perming agents on her things. Once Miss Jung learned San hadn't anyone else in the world, her mistreatment knew no bounds. Miss Jung was partially why San quit the salon. San hopes Su-ae isn't like Miss Jung. Then she smiles wryly to herself. Even though Miss Jung had been the one who harassed her the most, she's also the person San has thought about the most since she left the salon.

Throughout the day, they sell three pots, some lilies, twelve roses, and a basket of carnations and baby's breath. The customers ask for prices and flower names and stare at the owner when he replies on his notepad. They stare at San, too, who stands nearby. All afternoon, without ever giving her a direct order, the man teaches her how to work at the shop. He does this by doing something twice instead of once. San observes him from behind or helps him, thinking about the things she'll need to do here. There are hints of her own future in the way he waters the flowers or wraps the bouquets.

The day ends with the owner attaching the blue sash to a banyan tree as tall as San. It's past 9:00 p.m. He must be sorry about her first day ending so late because, with an apologetic expression, he writes, *Once Su-ae comes back, you can take turns leaving early.*

Memories of an Old Shirt

Yesterday, San walked the streets at night.

The streets at nighttime are as bright as during the day, thanks to the neon signage.

She walks up the way she came, but in the opposite direction: through the underground passageway that leads to Kyobo Bookstore, walking toward Gwanghwamun Gate and turning at the Hankook Ilbo building. Reentering the underground passage, she hesitates, seeing a group of teenage boys. They're almost dancing as they approach. Shaking their heads, thrusting their hips. Of the five, all but one or two wear earphones. One of them headbangs to whatever he's listening to. Each listening to different music, but walking together. They look ready to explode into rebellion at the slightest touch. Feeling eerily threatened, she stops in her tracks and stands still for a moment. She's ready to go back up the steps if need be. She stands there until the boys with baggy trousers and dyed hair gaggle by, and then she finally walks down to the passageway. There's no one there now that the boys have left. Yet even the emptiness frightens her, hastening her steps to the other side.

She comes upon the front gate of the museum, her eyes fixed on a café called Palette as she waits for the stoplight to change. When it does, she crosses the street. She glances at the bus station, where the 104 has arrived, and follows the path that leads to the Museum of Modern Art. Shadows of green ginkgo trees stretch before her on the pavement. Pale fluorescence from the streetlamps shines in between the fan shapes.

While she holds on to her bag strap with one hand, the tension from inside the underground passage disappears, and fatigue settles in. A man and a woman lean against the wall of the ancient palace across the street. That side is also covered in ginkgo-leaf shadows. Out of habit, she looks up at the night sky, and the sight of the crescent moon makes her pause.

Past the art museum, the streets grow narrow.

Here trees no longer line the avenue. Both the road and the sidewalk are tight. There are a few cafés: one with candlelight, one with its glass doors accordioned open. The scent of stir-fried tomatoes, onions, and sausage permeates the alley. San realizes she hasn't eaten anything all day except for some milk tea, and hunger overwhelms her. Gripping the strap of her bag, she walks faster and notices a pair of lovers inside a café with a little window.

The narrow street starts going uphill.

Farther up this street is her building with its long windows. From there the street divides into the Prime Minister's office and Samcheong Tunnel. There's always a policeman on duty at this fork. Back downhill leads to another tree-lined avenue.

Standing beneath the ginkgo across from her apartment, she looks up at her room. There are a pair of long windows, both unlit. The traditional paper-covered framing of the inner windows lends them a serene, templelike mood that seems out of place. There she is, staring up at her home. It feels like she's coming back after a long time gone, even though she only left that morning. She even misses the long room. The lights of the realtor's office are off, and of course those of the recreation office.

She thinks about the flower shop she has just left. It must be dark there now as well, with the lights off. Flowers and trees left to themselves. The lilies, balloon flowers, prairie gentians in their blue buckets—all bathed in darkness.

The streetlamps manage to avoid her room windows altogether. She doesn't wait for the signal as she crosses the street, mindful of the cars. It would be nice if she had someone to turn the lights on before she came back from work. In her heart, whenever she returns home late at night, there's always the hope that when she looks up from the street, someone will have turned on the lights for her. This has never once come to pass.

Once she's crossed the street, she goes inside to the bathroom and hangs up her bag and uses the toilet. The lights are off in the tiny living room of the inner annex. Walking up the shadowy steps, she almost slips twice. She prods about for the keyhole before unlocking her door. As soon as the door opens, she reaches for the light while taking off her shoes at the same time. How she has wanted to take them off all day. Now the window will shine brightly when seen from downstairs.

Once inside, she puts her bag down on top of the little refrigerator and opens the door. Two apple wedges and a winter melon, a plastic cup of peach yogurt, half a carton of milk, a block of tofu, preserved fish roe, a container of kimchi, and a bottle of water. She wants rice, so she closes the fridge, picks up the unwashed mug, and goes into the kitchen. Placing the mug in the sink, she takes out a handful of rice from the ten-kilogram bag under the sink, rinses it several times in running water, and readies the rice cooker. From a nearby basket, she also takes a potato and an onion and peels them, dropping the peels into the sink. She places an earthen pot with some water on the stove, and takes a lump of doenjang paste from a reddish-brown jar. She stirs the paste into the pot. She tosses in a handful of dried anchovies as she turns on the gas. As she unhooks a little table from the wall and unfolds its legs and sets down her utensils, the water begins to boil.

The fragrance of doenjang and anchovies fills the little kitchen. She always seeks out this smell whenever she is hungry. From time to time, whenever she wakes up in the middle of the night and her stomach feels a little empty, she might make a little bowl of this broth to drink before going back to sleep. Or when she has a headache, or digestive problems, especially stomach cramps, she will turn to this broth. It makes her smile in solitude. She fishes out the anchovies one by one from the bubbling stew.

Perhaps she should buy a little sieve to strain the anchovies. There's too much broth, so she's ladling some of it out and tossing the potatoes and onions in when someone calls out, "Miss!"

San leans out the door, ladle in hand.

The landlady, who raised her rent just that morning, stands there with her third and youngest daughter on her back. The little girl hands San piece of paper.

"She drew you in kindergarten."

"She drew me?"

"This little one thinks you're pretty. She wants to be like you."

Like me?

The landlady's unexpected words cause San to look back at the youngest daughter's face. The streetlamps near the Prime Minister's office illuminate her carefree smile. Suddenly shy, the girl turns her head away and rocks her feet. San strokes the child's hair and tucks away the drawing. She's still holding her ladle in her hand.

"Oh, and this—my children wanted pajeon so I fried some up, and I heard footsteps so I brought you one. And this is a letter."

A letter?

She takes both the plate of pajeon and the letter from her landlady.

"I just made it. Eat it before it gets cold." She turns to leave.

Looking up from trying to discern the name on the envelope, San calls out for her to wait.

"About the key money you mentioned this morning . . ."

The landlady pauses.

San falters despite having stopped the landlady. The child stares as she hesitates. Embarrassment overcomes San as she feels their doubled stare. Two million won. This meant two million won on top of the initial deposit and monthly rent she was already paying. Two whole million won. The bubbling sound of the boiling pot interrupts the silence growing between the three of them. The smell of doenjang seeps in between her hesitant self, the landlady, and the child. Still holding her ladle in one hand and a plate and a letter in the other, San takes a deep breath before speaking again.

"I was wondering if I could pay that in installments. Until I save enough money."

The landlady stares at her.

"I got a job today. I can start saving now." She's sweating as she says this.

"The thing is . . . my eldest child, she went into a piano store today to practice, and the shopkeeper kicked her out. She came home with her eyes red from crying. How trying it is to raise children! We must be the only house that has three daughters but no piano."

Now San has nothing to say.

"I know I'm asking a lot, but it's not like you won't get that money back. It's basically like saving it in a bank."

Saving.

The mention of "saving" depresses San. All throughout middle school and high school, adults drilled into her head that having savings was important. She regrets mentioning it at all. Regrets getting herself into a situation that's making her forehead bead with sweat.

"How much is your pay?" The landlady is asking about her pay before asking where she works.

"I don't know yet."

"You accepted a job without knowing your pay?"

San squirms in the direct, incredulous stare of her landlady. Indeed, she doesn't know. The only mention of money was San telling the florist that the pay at her last job had been ₩800,000. That probably wasn't going to be her pay. Working at a flower shop was a service job. Service jobs rarely paid well. When she first worked at the salon, she made ₩400,000 a month. Even when she got there by eight in the morning and left around ten at night. Even when she only took off the third Tuesday of every month and worked every holiday and weekend. In Seoul, famous hair salons branded themselves as "hair shops" instead of salons and invariably had branches in fashionable neighborhoods like Gangnam, Shinchon, or Myeong-dong. Aspiring hairstylists wanted to set up their own shops someday, which meant working for a reputable shop was more important than pursuing a higher salary. The fact that they had once worked in such places would be an important asset on their résumé. But for someone who had never gone to beauty school, it was all impossible. The only reason San could get a job as a salon assistant and survive for two years was purely because her mother had been a hairdresser. Despite having played with her mother's scissors and curling irons as a little child, it was only when San reached the end of her two-year apprenticeship that her pay reached ₩800,000. Her only additional income had been the occasional ₩5,000 or ₩10,000 tip customers tossed her way for manicures or facials.

But she has never worked at a flower shop before. Nothing she learned apprenticing at the hair salon will help her there.

San strokes the hair of the quiet listening child on her landlady's back and says, "All right. I'll figure something out."

The relieved landlady descends the steps. San, who accepted a job today without even discussing her pay, turns the envelope to the

light to see who has sent her a letter. Her eyes widen: Lee Mirae.
Lee Mirae? Mother? Mother sent a letter? She gently sets down the
ladle and plate and rips open the envelope then and there.

> *It's been a while.*
> *I'm back at the room you used to live in at Suwon.*
> *I've been here about a year.*
> *It took a long time to find you.*
> *Come visit whenever you can.*
> *Even just once.*
> *There's something I want to ask of you.*
> *I know you find it hard to forgive me.*
> *But I want to see you just one more time.*
> *Just once.*
> *Please, I beg you.*
>
> *From Lee Mirae*

San puts the letter back in the envelope and on a shelf in the
kitchen. *From Lee Mirae.* Both on the envelope and letter. Not one
mention of Mother or Mom or any other indication of maternity.
She was back in the Suwon room. Why? San is tight-lipped as she
sets the table. The doenjang stew has boiled down too much, so the
broth is dense and salty. San puts down a trivet, wraps the earthen
pot with a white cloth, and places it on the table. The landlady's
pajeon finds a place next to the pot. A little soy sauce dish, a plain
water cup, an unadorned rice bowl, and a spoon join the pot and
plate on the little table. She carries the table into her room. She
opens the electric rice cooker and loads up her rice bowl. A bit of
salted pollack roe from the fridge ends up in the soy sauce dish.
The bottle is opened and clear water is poured into the cup. Just as
she's about to sit down, she pulls up a legless chair, places it across
from her, and adds a straw hat hanging on the wall. She doesn't

want to eat alone. Having the straw hat there makes her think she's sitting with someone.

"I should go to the bank tomorrow," she muses to the straw hat. "It's probably less than half the target rate, but it'll be over a million won."

She brings a spoonful of the condensed stew to her lips. Too salty. She tries the pajeon, splitting off a piece with her chopsticks. It's a little bland. She brings a little more stew to her mouth. The effect is like eating doenjang-smeared pajeon. She frowns.

Taking a sip of water, she looks at the straw hat and mutters, "I don't know if I could get a loan."

While she chews, her thoughts squirm at the prospect of going to the bank tomorrow to close her half-filled savings account and inquire about loans.

"I wonder if I'll ever get to fill up an installment deposit instead of closing it midway." Her lips twist into a pout.

In the midst of her dinner, she looks up at the clock: 10:20. Too late to eat, she thinks, putting down her spoon.

She finishes preparing for bed and sits by an open window.

She's leaning back in a chair with her feet propped up on the small fridge. The glow from passing cars lingers on her face before vanishing. Each time this happens, the nighttime lotion applied on her pale skin gleams. Her colorless face, staring out at the unbothered ginkgo trees and the cafés behind them, appears and disappears with the light.

San wears an expression of melancholy, perhaps, but also of loneliness.

It is an expression that is not hers alone. A young woman on an escalator, a young man silently walking from building to building with a résumé in hand, salarymen on the subway at dawn—the same expression appears and disappears from their faces.

Presently, she stands up.

She walks the length of the apartment. There are sliding doors in the middle, an attempt to divide the space into a bedroom and living room. The room she's been sitting in with the fridge is the living room, and the inner room that she's walking into now is the bedroom. The bedroom and kitchen are connected by a door. In the kitchen, she takes out her mug and mixes herself some iced tea, goes back the way she came, and sits down in the same way. Leaning back, feet propped up, eyes staring into the night. The slightly bitter taste of the tea rests on the tip of her tongue. Two drunk people come out of the café, only to be dragged back in by a third who refuses to see them go; she watches the scene as if it's happening on a faraway screen.

To her, the café is no longer a real place but part of a stage. No matter what happens there, it will only be scenery. Despite the season, there are lit candles inside. Perhaps it's a fad to always have candles on café tables now. This silly thought makes her smile wanly and think, What a long day it's been. The events of the morning feel like they happened ten days ago or more.

She places the mug on top of the fridge and gets up. From a desk in a corner of the long room, she picks up a book and notebook. Moving the mug to the windowsill, she places the book and notebook on the fridge. The book has been in her possession for a long time. It's been leafed through again and again, and has a tattered cover. Wedged in its pages is a fountain pen—a writing implement people rarely use nowadays. It leaves only impressions, not letters; she twists it open and takes a look inside before walking back to the desk to bring out a bottle of blue Pilot ink. The lid refuses to open. Even with a dry dishrag around it, the lid doesn't budge. She puts it down and stares, not knowing what to do. Her palms are red from her exertions.

She hears someone coming up the steps. The footsteps stop at the top of the stairs. The sound of keys being fished out of a pocket.

Someone is unlocking the door to the recreation office across from her room. Only ever having seen a locked door, this is the first time she's had any indication whatsoever of a real neighbor. She swiftly picks up the ink bottle, goes to her door, and swings it open.

A young man is trying to unlock the recreation office. He's wearing a khaki-colored shirt and white shorts that reach just below his knees, and he turns to San when her door opens. San sees an electric guitar case hanging from his shoulder and a dog sticking next to him as closely as his guitar. The dog is shaggy and unshorn, and seems to be out of breath from climbing the stairs; it pants, black eyes peeking out at her from underneath white fur. She suddenly regrets having burst so abruptly out onto the landing, but it's too late now. The young man is already looking at her expectantly.

She hands the Pilot ink bottle to this man she's never met before. "My bottle won't open."

The young man, his hair dyed with red highlights, stares at her as if to say, So what do you want me to do about it? She's never seen his face before. Of course, she's never seen the door to the recreation office open at all. His eyes are rebellious. Not only that—his expression is resentful. There's a shadow beneath his prominent nose.

"Could you open it for me?"

Expression unchanging, the young man takes the bottle from her and examines it.

The lid that had refused to budge opens effortlessly. So effortlessly that it embarrasses her to have made such a fuss. As she accepts the bottle from him, she mumbles, "How strange, it didn't open before." The young man takes his guitar and his dog into the opened office and slams the door shut without a word.

San stands there for a moment with the ink bottle.

The narrow staircase is dark. The glow from her opened door shines like a spotlight. It's like a scene from a play. She takes a moment to placate the hurt from the slammed door and ignored thanks, then she silently moves back into her room and closes the door. Her face is pale again as she fills the fountain pen on the fridge with ink.

For a long time, she sits there with the ink-filled pen in her hand.

The notebook is spread open, and she begins to copy sentences from the tattered book. Back when she dreamed of quitting the hair salon and becoming a word processor operator, she would use this book for typing practice. It had been a coincidence that a poster of the author's face had been hanging near the entrance of the publisher where she'd interviewed. She pokes softly at an inner loneliness trembling within her as she presses the fountain pen to a blank page and copies word for word.

> When I was younger, they say I never went anywhere without a certain old shirt of my mother's. I wound that shirt around my fist when I breastfed, and would only sleep when that shirt was spread under me. Around the time I began to walk, I would always stop to grab the shirt before stumbling toward whoever was calling for me. Even when I tripped over that shirt, I did not whine or cry. Who knew when I developed such an attachment to it or why it had to be that shirt, but seeing as I can still remember its soft texture, I believe I carried it with me until I was six or seven. I didn't cry or fuss much as a child, except for one instance, when they tried to take my shirt away from me.

That's how much she has copied when she sits back in her chair. Flipping pages, she stares at the author's photograph on the ragged front flap. San has looked at it so many times she feels she knows the author personally. Once again, she brings pen to paper.

According to my second older brother (who always carried me on his back), he was taking care of me one summer day when I seemed especially attached to the shirt. Annoyed that I was biting at it until my lips were red, and at the heat stifling his back, he made to take it away from me. When tantrums and kicking weren't enough to get it back, I started to bite and slam my head against my brother's back, throwing such a tantrum that I ran out of breath. My brother thought I had died then—a baby foaming at the mouth and yellow in the face, refusing to breathe. From then on, it seems that no one made an issue about my carrying around that shirt.

San sits there, intently copying each sentence.

Nothing can distract her now, whatever might happen outside. As she copies each line, her left index finger following along the page, she never once looks out the open window.

My mother reminisced how my dependence on the shirt increased by the day, and on days when she had to work in the fields and there was no babysitter, she would simply leave me asleep in an empty room with the shirt, and I'd be rolling around with it by the time she got back. Rubbing my face or my hands in it, or sucking at it.

Sometimes, I find myself remembering that shirt as if I were looking into someone else's secret.

Around the time I turned thirty, I lived with my younger sister near the Seodaemun Prison in a singles' apartment built like a jail cell. Three years apart in age, my sister and I went to a jeweler's by the prison and bought a gold necklace for her and a 14K ring for me, purchases toward an auspicious future. I don't know what happened to my sister's necklace but I cherished that ring. When I saw a relationship near its death, when my pride was hurt, or whenever I felt anxious or desperate, I would unconsciously fondle that ring. When I had to pick a side, or found myself suffering the urge to destroy something, I would twist the ring on my finger. That fidgeting allowed me not to make a fuss. It allowed me not to express violence. This ring I had for seven years just disappeared without my ever remembering where I had taken it off. Being one of my few jewels, I'd rarely removed it from my hand. Now there's only the groove it left on my finger. How I searched for days. Once I accepted it was lost for good, it felt like my heart had been emptied. Like seven years of my life were gone.

Six months have passed, and I still find myself looking for it from time to time.

Sometimes, I wonder if I'm a bad person. Usually when I feel twisted about inside. A sense of endless distraction finds me lying prostrate on the floor. My ungoverned hurt manifests as aches all over my body. A bad person is someone who makes it impossible to long for them. Their heads feel like bursting, their shoulders ache, and their legs are drained of strength. They'll spend a day prostrate, maybe even a week. Until they hear a pop in their heart. Until they think there is nothing more to lose. Until they walk back the long way they came in solitude. That is the person I am, someone who hurts the one who hurt me until they too hear a pop in their hearts. This realization fills me, every time, with sorrow.

And to experience this process of realization every time is also horrifying. Despite thinking I could maybe skip a few steps or find the process easier with experience, I am still repeating it; nothing about me will change, I have to cut the telephone line connecting me to the outside world in order to conceal the words that threaten to burst forth, I must use all of these passive methods of isolation as treatment.

While I worked on a novella, after an almost yearlong

*hiatus from writing, memories of that shirt and ring kept rising
and falling completely unprompted. Perhaps I'm wrong; sometimes, when I stare out the window into the parking lot at
dawn where not a soul passes by, countless moving images
superimpose themselves in my mind. The kind of footage
empty common spaces inspire, places like a valley stream that
flows even while we sleep, highways with zooming cars, flowers
blooming, fishing boats tied up at docks, the blind depths of
oceans, empty audience seats at night, dark and strange muse-
ums, stairwells of skyscrapers, apartments filled with boxes but
empty of people, how one must hide and put away the footage, the ephemera. Perhaps the moments I captured might
find meaning as places of nothingness.*

*The morning's calm as I come back from the shops, my
face swollen from lack of sleep.*

*You said so, you did so, you almost ran out of breath, you
relied on it for seven years—what did you do with that shirt,
with that ring. How could you have parted from them with
no farewell ritual, with such little emotion. No one tells me
about what happened after. I don't remember myself. What
color or pattern was the shirt, what material or cut. The groove
my ring had made on my hand is long gone. Where I had
taken it off, why I had taken it off, I remember nothing. Just
a little bit of the scent and feeling of that shirt . . . after it had
watched over and comforted you for seven years throughout
the deaths of your relationships.*

What say you, this forgetfulness, this emptiness.

She copies that final sentence, draws a line, writes the title
"Memories of an Old Shirt," and looks down at the blue letters writ-
ten neatly on the page. Writing allows San to hide herself in words.
Her dream is to become someone who writes. Nothing would make

her more grateful than the opportunity to do so. The thought of writing in a better setting puts butterflies in her stomach. In her imagination, a better setting is: a wide room where no one can intrude, with a big table in that room. The bigger the table, the better, she thinks. She wouldn't have to reshelve her books all the time, she could eat her dinner on a corner of it, and sometimes, she might even take a nap on top of it . . . When she thinks of herself writing on such a big table in a wide-open room, she feels like perhaps life is worth living. But right now, she copies out sentences on top of a minifridge. She caps her fountain pen and sets it down. Is it because of the writing? Or the sentences? Her face spreads into a smile, with a relief that has been missing all day.

Su-ae

July marks the true beginning of summer.

After Su-ae returns to work, the shop owner—the one who hired San—no longer shows up. While this strikes San as odd, Su-ae takes it in stride. All she says is, He's my uncle. His real work is at the farm in Gupabal. Su-ae has a slightly long face and mischievous dimples. Short bangs tremble on her forehead. When she walks, she shimmies her small behind. San hadn't even mentioned it but Su-ae says, loud and clear, Look, I know I have a duck butt, it's not like I'm trying to walk this way, and there's nothing I can do about it. Despite not wearing lip gloss, Su-ae's lips are as red as the China pinks. She's short and skilled with her hands.

Su-ae is disarming from the start, treating San as if they were old friends. This is why San dares to ask her to be a guarantor for a bank loan. But in the end, San doesn't even need to take out a loan; Su-ae, who had been sleeping in a little room inside the flower shop, packs her things and moves in with San, handing over the two million won as her share of the key money. Su-ae's move marks the end of San living in a room of her own, much less getting the table of her dreams. But at least she didn't have to close her install-ment savings, even if she hadn't put in any money for a while. The new black piano is too big for any of the bedrooms, so it's placed in their landlady's living room instead. Now the eldest daughter can play the piano whenever she wants, at dawn or late at night.

When San had known only Su-ae's name and had wondered what she might look like, she had assumed Su-ae would be older; they are, in fact, the same age. They met for the first time one morning as Su-ae came into the shop, arriving from the farm in Gupabal bearing bushels of sea lavenders, peonies, and hydrangea bushes, greeting San brightly as if they'd met a hundred times before. Su-ae switched to the informal register as soon as she discovered neither was older than the other. Within a week, they were roommates. On their first night living together, they bought a tiny cake from Paris Baguette, lit it with candles, and congratulated each other. It was Su-ae's suggestion, and San acquiesced. They even bought a bottle of Majuang Mosel for a toast.

Su-ae liked San's long room on sight. She stuck her head out of the window and exclaimed, "Those ginkgo trees are going to be mighty yellow in the fall!," adding that they should go to the café sometime to have a beer. San had only observed the café across the street, never once thinking of going in herself, but here Su-ae was dreaming of café evenings on her first day.

San now has a roommate.

At night, they draw an invisible line through the apartment, with San sleeping on the far side of the long room. Su-ae sleeps by the fridge on the small bed she used at the flower shop. During the day, the bed serves as a place to sit for both of them. Sometimes, when San watches Su-ae sleeping facedown on the bed, a smile tugs at the corners of her lips. Petite Su-ae sleeping in her bed reminds San of a ladybug clinging desperately to a tree trunk.

Su-ae wakes up at dawn, always before San. Even when she falls asleep after midnight, her eyes automatically open around five in the morning, and she moves quietly so as not to wake her roommate. But despite Su-ae's consideration, San eventually begins to go to bed an hour earlier than when she lived alone. Getting up so early made San feel dazed at first, but now she's used to it. Within a week, she's also started breakfasting on Baskin Robbins mint chocolate chip ice cream. When San asked Su-ae what was up with the ice cream, Su-ae replied, No good reason. She had opened her refrigerator one morning and discovered the only thing in it was Baskin Robbins mint chocolate chip ice cream, and that has been her breakfast ever since. Su-ae claims if she didn't have her morning dose, her insides would feel off all day.

When it comes to tending flowers and plants, Su-ae's handiwork is masterful. Her experience is obvious despite her youth. Whenever they have time, Su-ae, with her small behind sticking out, teaches San how to care for plants like monsteras and lady palms. Su-ae's knowledge makes her seem elegant and efficient, like a flower-arranging master. Ever since San and Su-ae began living together, their breakfasts have been mint chocolate chip ice cream. They eat lunch at the Sapporo Udon House, or order delivery sashimi-topped rice, or kimbap, or spicy noodles. They take turns going home earlier to cook each other dinner in the small kitchen. After, they soak their swollen feet and watch the television Su-ae brought with her, or listen to the sound of the landlord's eldest daughter practicing until they drift off to sleep. Sometimes, they'll go to the mountain springs at Samcheong Park.

The pansies, marigolds, forget-me-nots, primroses, and daisies that had ruled the flower shop up until early summer are replaced by touch-me-nots, zinnias, cockscombs, and sunflowers. The deeper it gets into the season, the more brilliant the flowers become. Satiny white gardenia flowers unfurl between luscious green leaves, and the queen-of-the-night cactus bursts into spectacular fuchsia blossoms. The sight of the bellflowers blooming all at once takes San's breath away. She can almost hear the sound of bells softly chiming around her.

The most popular flowers of the season are the lilies of the valley.

Stemming from two overlapping leaves, the little cups blossom with their heads bowed down. Their shyness is impossible to ignore, and San often finds herself staring at them. Sometimes, San picks out wilting nasturtium flowers and puts them on her tongue. With the paper-thin petals sitting in her mouth, she admires the dark pink gloxinias gleaming like velvet.

San's still gaze is serene.

San had first seen *Wanted: A woman to look after flowers* and had promptly fled. Now, as she takes in the plants, she can't conjure what she felt back then at all. That repulsion toward having a job out on the street—that's what had made her run. But now as she regards the gloxinias she seems content with her place in the flower shop. Her previous determination, to spend only a month or two there before getting an office job, fades as she looks around.

But once San's eyes leave the plants, her gaze goes blank. Her line of sight is filled with busy pedestrians. A placard advertising a new performance jerks in the wind against its ropes. The parked cars look bored as they sizzle in the sun. The sycamore leaves, as big as hands, go limp in the afternoon heat.

San's fingers no longer tap *I am waiting for the bus* as she waits at the stop. The San who typed *I am riding the bus* on her lap seems to have disappeared. Not to mention the San who would spread open a notebook and copy sentences. Her notebook is gathering a layer of dust. The Pilot ink in her fountain pen is drying up. The ink bottle she had gotten open with such difficulty is closed again, neglected in a corner.

San's empty stare moves over the objects of the outside world, not settling anywhere until they return to the gloxinias.

When San collects water to shower the pavement in front of the shop, Su-ae exclaims, "You're doing that again?" San had already done it half an hour ago. Ignoring Su-ae, San goes out and sprinkles water on the flowers outside. She squeezes a rag and wipes the windows. The windows and pavement eagerly suck in moisture. Witnessing the already-dry street makes her feel like she's going to crack. The flowers look like they're panting when there are no beads of water on the window.

When San does this, her empty expression—the one that looks as if she's thinking, Why does nothing ever happen—fades for a moment. The look from when she's looking at the gloxinias returns. Maybe . . .

Taking care of the plants might be a kind of consolation for her sinking heart, for the feeling that she's losing out on her dreams. Perhaps whenever she wipes the window or sprinkles the plants exposed out on the street, it's her own fragile inner self that she's watering.

Every Monday and Friday, Su-ae puts on a hat and goes out to the farm in Gupabal. Occasionally she will go to the wholesale florists' to bring back carnations and roses, but she only does that on occasion, and it's mostly from the farm that they get their plants and herbaceous flowers and even pots and other equipment. Su-ae tells San, "It's really rare for a retail shop to do that. It's only possible because Uncle happens to run a farm."

There are also things that are only possible because of Su-ae.

Su-ae, who has just turned twenty-three.

Su-ae projects a sort of toughness that suggests she'll never be hurt. This probably wasn't her personality to start. Su-ae affects a jaded cynicism that hints she's seen too much of the world. To San, Su-ae's strength feels magical. Su-ae knows how to say, in a very clear voice, No. I don't think so. When the landlady came up with the water and electricity bill, Su-ae told her, No, I don't think so. We're hardly at home during the day. Making us pay half for the utilities isn't fair. The landlady said, The recreation office has no tap and that girl over there has paid half until now, pointing to San. Su-ae replied, Whatever you've done until now, I don't think so, this isn't right. What a bold young lady you are, the land-lady said as she went back down the stairs, and from then on she divided the utility fees differently. Thanks to Su-ae, San went from being responsible for half the utility bills to just a third. Su-ae was adept in handling financial affairs. She paid exactly half of San's decreased bills.

Not only could Su-ae say, I don't think so, but she could also tell the landlord's family, Please be quiet!

The landlord and landlady often fight fierce battles that make it seem like divorce is imminent. When San first moved into the apartment and heard their fights, she was so scared that she covered her head with her blanket. When the daughters burst into tears, the landlord would shout, Shut your mouths! Which would only make them cry harder. When he was shouting, the man looked less like a father but more like an intruder. If the girls wouldn't stop crying he would yell, You useless bitches!, going on about how he didn't have a son to take to the bathhouse, that all the females in the family were suffocating him. And in the morning, San would catch a glimpse of the family having breakfast like nothing had happened and wonder, Did I hear things? Eventually she got used to it and learned to ignore the fights. She only hoped that they didn't happen too often. And one day, she was absently listening to the fighting downstairs. As usual the husband burst out into the street and began smashing the folding tables stacked in the corridor. The tea tables, the two-person tables, the four-person ones—San was used to hear-ing them shatter on the pavement. Just when she thought it was time for the three daughters to start crying, sure enough, she heard the three daughters crying. Su-ae, who had been applying mois-turizer, opened the kitchen door, stood at the top of the stairs, and shouted, Would you please keep it down!

The landlord's family—who had never heard a peep from San the whole time she lived there—fell into an amazed silence and stared up into the dark stairwell. They were staring in the general direction of Su-ae, who had clearly shouted, Would you please keep it down! After a brief moment, when the landlord finally understood it had been the new girl, he shouted, Get out of my house! Su-ae snapped back, You signed a contract, we have a right to live here until it runs out!

San was nothing if not hesitant. Su-ae had no hesitation whatsoever. When she wanted to laugh, she laughed. She was bold to the point of aggressive. Was it her firmness of manner, or her clear and calm voice? And yet there was nothing vulgar about her boldness; it was even beautiful. Anyone with a bit of insight might have guessed that Su-ae's personality came from some kind of lack. Just as San's endlessly hesitant personality was a different kind of lack. And that excessive hesitation and excessive boldness were really part of the same story.

On the days Su-ae goes to the Gupabal farm, San is alone in the flower shop.

Su-ae gets to the farm by bus, but she returns riding a small truck. The driver is not the man who hired San. San assumes this young man works at the farm. He parks the truck on the curb, carefully off-loads the striped dracaenas and ficus bonsai trees, and drives off. That's it. He gently carries even the smallest geranium pot into the shop without ever saying a word, ignoring San's polite greeting. He ignores her nod goodbye when he climbs back behind the steering wheel of the truck to drive away. The first time it happens, San mumbles, "I guess he's mute . . ." as she gathers the trowels and earth needed to repot the freshly uprooted and vinyl-wrapped plants.

Su-ae answers, "He isn't. He just listens to only Uncle, and conveys what Uncle says."

"What do you mean?"

"He's Uncle's ears and voice."

San waits for Su-ae to continue.

"We grew up together on the farm. Someone abandoned him at the gates of Uncle's farm. Uncle ended up raising him."

As San looks wordlessly at her, Su-ae adds, "I was abandoned by my mother, too, actually." She says it like it is nothing to her.

"I was thrown away, basically. What kind of parent dies when there's a two-year-old to take care of? Don't you think so?" She looks back at San as if challenging her. "I know it was an accident, but how could she do that? Leave behind her daughter who couldn't even talk?"

Because Su-ae looks like she might knock San's eyes out if she doesn't agree, San manages to say, "Oh, yes."

"So I decided to exact my revenge. By ruining my life. She's not here anymore, but if she's watching me from somewhere, I didn't want to give her the satisfaction of seeing me live a good life. I wanted to ruin what life I had left."

She grins, and adds, "So I ran away from the farm. I dropped out of school and roamed the streets at night. I did that for two years but Uncle never gave up on trying to find me. It's harder than you think to ruin your life."

Su-ae clams up after that. She spreads the composted leaves, river sand, and red granite soil on the floor with more attention than usual. As if she hasn't said what she said. Her mouth is shut so hard that her jaw goes practically square.

Never having seen Su-ae like this before, San finds herself unable to help or to do any other work; she just stands there, watching Su-ae's rapidly moving hands. Su-ae sifts the granite soil and rubs the leaf compost across the net to even out its texture. Only then does she look up at San.

"The granite soil is the base. Just think of the proportions of it, the compost, and the sand as six to three to one. Five liters of the soil mix is five pots. Small ones."

San follows Su-ae's lead as she plants pansies and poinsettias into seven pots. The work seems to calm Su-ae. She asks San if she's ever seen papaya palms.

Papaya palms?

When San says no, Su-ae says that she has, and whispers as if telling a big secret: "Uncle went to Indonesia six months ago and brought back some ficus bonsai. You might not recognize them at first. When they're brought in, they're just blocks of wood. But you put them in the greenhouse and eventually, leaves sprout. It's amazing! They were doing well when I looked in today. I bet you would've liked them. Green leaves on three thousand ficus bonsai standing in line, fluttering in the breeze. There's no forest quite like that. Just spectacular. The ones he put outside the greenhouse for more sun were really grand. But there were a couple of trees I couldn't recognize, off to the side. They were so different, I immediately spotted them. Standing a meter apart, with three identically spaced leaves on each. Uncle told me they were papaya. When I asked him if they were imports, he said the papaya seeds had slipped in when the ficus came in. So he'd planted them, and one day, there they grew."

"..."

"Don't you want to see them?"

"..."

"I said, don't you want to see them?"

"I want to see them."

"Then let's go together the next time."

That day, Su-ae, as if remembering something, plants oregano, lavender, lemon balm, mint, and some other herbs in a long white planter. She hands the planter to San as she leaves work first.

"Put this in the room. It smells good, and you can rip off a leaf to chew when you have indigestion." After a moment of hesitation, she adds, "Don't wait for me tonight, have dinner without me."

San puts the planter on the windowsill. Thinking Su-ae had only meant she would have dinner on her own and not that she wouldn't come home at all, San waits for Su-ae all night. Just as she had done before Su-ae moved in, she opens the windows and stares out into the street. There's an exceptional number of insects clinging to the window screen, but Su-ae does not come home even at dawn. When San arrives at the flower shop the next morning, Su-ae has already finished the morning cleanup.

"What happened?" San asks.

To which Su-ae replies, "I told you to have dinner without me."

Twenty-Three

On the seventeenth of July, San turns twenty-three.

In the interim, the herbs in the planter have grown thick and lush, filling up the windowsill. Now the two women wake up every morning to their scent. On San's twenty-third birthday, she reads a newspaper story about a young man who got drunk and murdered his parents with a hammer. The man in the photo has his head bowed low. The article said that he was obsessed with movies and had confessed to killing his parents the same way he saw in a film. He'd been abused by his parents since childhood, and when they had refused to support his studies after he'd been discharged from military service, he had gone drinking until dawn. When he realized what he had done, it was too late.

Unable to read anymore, San folds the morning paper three times. Leaving the bathroom at the bottom of the stairwell, she pushes the paper under the landlady's door and climbs the stairs.

Su-ae is now in the habit of going swimming every morning. She jogs to a pool in Jae-dong. Even if Su-ae makes every shortcut possible through the twisting alleys, the trip takes at least twenty minutes. When she returns, her cheeks are flushed and her short hair smells of floral shampoo.

Su-ae wants San to join her but San demurs. It is probably the first time San has said no to Su-ae. No doubt Su-ae will look for mint chocolate chip ice cream that morning, but instead San boils seaweed soup and delicately washes rice so the embryo buds don't fall off the grains. On her way home last night, San had bought dried croaker at the basement market in Nagwon Instrument Arcade. The fish is cooking in a pan.

Her mother used to do this.

San always knew it was her birthday by this smell—the seaweed soup and croaker. She thinks she was happy, lying in bed, smelling that aroma. Later on, it turned into something else. Her mother made these dishes on a day that wasn't her birthday. Sitting San down at the carefully set table, her mother told her she was leaving. That she was sorry, but she had no other choice. Seaweed soup and croaker on days that weren't San's birthday made her wince. Because whenever her mother needed to make an important decision or do something drastic, she would make seaweed soup and croaker for San.

Every time her mother tried to start anew with someone, he failed her.

The first time was with a young man, a seasonal worker who tilled the fields. He had hired San's mother for a perm and fallen for her, and her mother, reluctant at first, had eventually accepted his affections and left the village with him when the migrant workers moved on. The morning she left San behind in the rented room, her mother made rice, seaweed soup, and croaker for her breakfast. San had no words but her mother was in tears. The woman left her in that room. San finished her food and stared at the minari field as she walked to school. She did her homework, washed her clothes, wiped the floor, pulled her blanket to her neck, and went to sleep alone. Then one day, she found her mother waiting for her at home.

Her mother moved them to the city of Suwon. And between then and when San entered her first year of high school, her mother would cook seaweed soup four more times on days that weren't her birthday. San's mother would sit her down and tell her she had to leave. There was nothing for San to say.

Her mother. San thinks about her from time to time.

If she had begged her to stay, in front of that carefully prepared food, would her mother have listened? Why had San never once tried to hold her back? Wherever it was that her mother went, she never forgot to send her daughter money for school until San graduated.

The last time San had seen her mother was when she was a freshman in high school.

The croaker on the table was particularly fleshy. It's a real Yeonggwang croaker, her mother had said, gloomy. San was somewhat used to her mother's goodbyes by now, and wished that even if she ended up coming back again, her mother would find some happiness in the interim. It couldn't be easy for her mother, either, leaving her child behind. San even thought the croaker was unnecessarily expensive, given that her mother would be back soon enough. But that had been the last time. Her mother left, and never came back. She'd gone to some man who had an orchard some-where, and he sent San money until she graduated high school, and that was all. There were occasional traces of her mother having come back to the house—there would be side dishes in the fridge or the room would have been cleaned—but San never sat down to have a meal with her mother again. She couldn't help hoping her mother would show up to her graduation, but she didn't. San left the school gates alone, watching families take photos in the falling snow and gift each other bouquets and head toward restaurants.

Su-ae would've called what San did next revenge.

The night of her high school graduation, San moved from Suwon to Seoul and left her mother no word. Perhaps "escaped" is a better way of putting it than "moved." That was already five years ago. Four birthdays, making rice and boiling seaweed soup and frying croaker without her mother.

Revenge?

Twenty-three years old today, San smiles sadly into the soup.

Leaving her mother no word . . . That's how San put it in her head. For all she knew, her mother had never once looked for her. Remembering the letter, she looks toward the shelf. She's back in the Suwon room? San's lips clamp tightly. With the paddle, she turns the cooked rice, thinking, I will never go back to her.

On her return, Su-ae just stops herself from saying, What's this? and instead opens her eyes wide at the food.

"It's my birthday today. Will you eat with me?"

"It's your birthday?"

"Yes."

"Why didn't you say anything?"

"What would you have done?"

"I would've made the seaweed soup for you, of course."

"And not go swimming?"

"You've got a point there."

Su-ae, whom San had expected to refuse her birthday meal in favor of mint chocolate chip ice cream, sits down and enthusiastically slurps broth. She even debones the croaker with her hands to make it easier to eat. It's so good . . . It's so good . . . she can't stop remarking.

"Hey, let's have some fun tonight."

"With what?"

"Leave it to me. Let's have a really good time. Should I call Mr. Choi?"

"Mr. Choi?"

"Choi Hyun-li, I mean."

San is quiet.

"Look at that face—I'm kidding! But why do you hate him so much?"

"I just do."

"Why?"

"I hate his eyes."

"His eyes?"

"The way they look at me."

Choi is an unavoidable regular at the flower shop.

He frequently commissions plants and flowers, adorned with script-bearing banners and ribbons, to be sent to Samseong-dong, Seogyo-dong, or the Press Center. Just as San had been told by the Gupabal farm owner, Su-ae loathes writing the calligraphy on the ribbons. She leaves San to do the writing. San asked how she did it before; Su-ae replied she simply took the ribbons to her uncle for him to take care of. And on busy days, Choi Hyun-li himself would write the words.

"He looks at you that way because he wants to sleep with you."

It's the casual way Su-ae says this that strikes San silent.

"He looked at Miss Choi that way, too."

"Miss Choi?"

"The unni who worked here before you."

"What happened?"

"It looked like they were going out for a while but then she suddenly quit, and we haven't seen her since."

Choi Hyun-li, meanwhile, drops by the flower shop from time to time, even when he has no business for them.

Have you had lunch? Isn't there a movie you want to see? A place you want to go to? Choi keeps asking her things, unperturbed by her lack of answers. Su-ae jumps in and says, I haven't had lunch. Have you seen *Through the Olive Trees* yet? I really want to visit Seokmo Island. Choi must pick up on Su-ae's mocking tone, but his eyes keep lingering on San. This only makes San grow more and more quiet. She can't understand her own aversion to Choi. His hair is always cropped like an athlete's, and he persists, as if her increasingly stiff posture is some unbearably adorable act she's putting on for him. He tells her to let him know anytime there's something she wants to eat, a movie she wants to see, or any place she wants to go.

On their way to the flower shop, the two women run into the young man coming out of the recreation office. The very one who opened San's ink bottle. He looks like he's spent the night in the office. The dog San saw before is there. In the brief awkwardness that ensues, Su-ae says, "Hey, did you know it's her birthday today? Do you want to hang out with us tonight?"

Mortified, San pokes Su-ae's side.

The young man gives them an annoyed look and is about to descend when Su-ae says, "Excuse me, did you hear what I just said? It's her birthday! We live right next door to each other and we've never even said hello!" Her tone is almost accusatory.

The young man smiles and says, "I have no time tonight, but if you chicks are bored later, come knock."

He quickly makes his way down to the bathroom in a rush. Eager to keep up with its owner, the dog follows suit. Had she been sharing a bathroom with that man this whole time? The thought makes San uneasy, but Su-ae is already down the stairs and walking out onto the street.

Later, the sun sets while they work.

Su-ae wears an apron and holds a pair of pruning shears. She's about to carefully trim the curved branches of a star jasmine bonsai. The apron is stained red and green from brushing against flowers and leaves. Sitting next to the steel table is San. On the desk is a book with a red cover titled *Wreaths and Flower Arranging* as well as a *Buena Vista Social Club* soundtrack CD. The book has always been there, but the CD is new. Su-ae bought it at Kyobo Bookstore on her way back from an errand. Smiling, she said it was the first time she had gifted anyone a CD. San has never received music for her birthday, either. When San shyly slips the CD out of the plastic bag, Su-ae says, "I happened to be passing by when I heard it and I liked their sound. The singers are old people, apparently."

Old people.

San rips open the shrink-wrapping. There's no CD player in the apartment. But there's a small boombox in the shop, which is where she inserts the disc. As the songs play, she looks through the translated lyrics in the liner notes. *Flowers sleep in my garden. Gladiolas and roses and lilies. And my sorrowful soul.*

Twenty-three years old today, San's hands hold a patterned rag used to wipe the table before and after arranging flowers. After multiple washes, it's dried into a soft square that she now folds into thirds. Su-ae insists they have to celebrate San turning twenty-three and is determined to close the shop at 8:30. On any other day, one of them would've gone to the apartment in Samcheong-dong first and prepared dinner. But now Su-ae suggests they eat out at some awesome place.

"An awesome place?"

"Like the Sky Lounge at the Plaza Hotel." Su-ae grins. "You don't want to? Oh good, I've never been there myself. I was worried for a minute that you'd say yes. But there's got to be someplace where the scene is hot."

Where the scene is hot. Su-ae's words bring a grin to San's face. San says she received a call from a friend during the day and she has to go see them. Surprised, Su-ae asks about this friend.

"Someone I used to work with at the hairdresser's," San replies.

Su-ae pouts and says, "Why can't I join you?"

Su-ae puts down the pruning shears and goes to the bathroom still wearing her stained apron.

San picks up the scissors. They have handles curved like fern fronds and San snips off a piece of the star jasmine bonsai, like Su-ae did. She examines the shears closely. Somehow the act of cutting leaves or branches makes her uncomfortable, but she does like the shears. They make snipping off any stem as simple as one-two. It's effortless. The flower shop has several kinds of shears: thinning shears with a vine-like curl of a wire connecting the handles, a pair with a looped handle to slip one's fingers in, and the general-purpose pruning shears she's holding.

Su-ae comes back, and they move on to repotting.

With expert swiftness, Su-ae picks out the plants that haven't grown properly, the ones with fallen flowers, and ones so overgrown they've ruined their shape. Whenever she bends over, San catches a glimpse of the small of her back. The soft bumps of vertebrae are like tree roots. It's the more exotic plants that adapt to repotting with ease. In the summer, rubber figs and palms prefer shade with filtered sunlight. They grow quickly near blinds or lace curtains. Too much direct sunlight turns the edges of their leaves brown. On the other hand, an excess of humidity can easily bring white fungus to their leaves and stems.

"This is what comes of excess!" Su-ae declares as she shows San the rotting leaves and stems of a short lady palm. "Look here, Miss Oh San. You've overwatered this poor plant."

Su-ae separates the palm's stems and prepares a pot with river-bed sand for good drainage. She says, "I'm not sure if it'll survive; it's not the right season for repotting."

Taking Su-ae's words to heart, San places the roots of the lady palm in the new pot with extra care. A smaller plant and well-suited for indoor life, lady palms are popular and there are many in the shop. At first, San thought "lady palm" was another word for bamboo. After learning they grew in the tropics of South America and Africa, she touched one of the narrow leaves to her cheek. They were one of the smaller exotic species at the flower shop, and she could never have imagined their homeland was so far away. San tended to give more water to the plants she was interested in. That became a problem. When perfectly healthy plants began to drop their petals or buds, Su-ae would say, That's because you've overwatered them; if you love things too much, they die. She said the same thing when the spider plant's long blades turned yellow.

There are scale bugs on the lady palm's stem.

Scale bugs are protected by a hard exoskeleton, making them impervious to pesticides. Su-ae, careful not to injure the plant, deftly scrapes off the bugs. Only when that doesn't work do they resort to pesticides. Su-ae reasons that plants probably do not like pesticides. But San is not good at scraping the bugs off and keeps hurting the plant, at which point Su-ae takes it away from her. In one easy move, she sweeps the offenders off the lady palm's stem and flicks them onto the floor.

San mixes the fertilizer and sprinkles some on the lady palm. Her face feels hot.

San has calmed down as she's gotten used to working in the shop. When she pots and fertilizes plants from the farm, she prays for their roots to grow as well as they did in the ground.

Inside the shop, San still feels as if she's working out on the street. But the green shine of her charges helps her forget her regrets, or gently buries clumps of memories she'd rather not untangle. Yet sometimes, even after a day of covering roots in palm mulch, she finds herself unable to sleep. Even after she's extracted all the soil from underneath her fingernails and her fatigue is so profound her back might snap in two, she's haunted by visions of the flower shop. As she lies there tossing and turning, she's surrounded by the panting of the roots she's planted, *hu hu*—, as they grow into their new home.

Now she steps out of the shop after saying to Su-ae, See you later.

San has taken off her apron and taken out her hairpins, and her black hair falls beneath her collar and sways as she walks. Her dress, patterned with white droplets, has a very worn hem. Several rips and tears have clearly been mended by hand. Her thin calves appear and disappear. When she walks, the droplets ride up her leg and bend at her knee. Her white sandals, more appropriate for beach holidays, float below her dress, their slight straps barely supporting her toes. She carries a transparent plastic bag with rope handles over her shoulder. The contents of the bag are completely visible: a white handkerchief folded in fourths, a coin purse made of persimmon-dyed cloth, and the CD.

When she's a few steps out the door, Su-ae comes after her. She drags San to the nearby Paris Baguette where she buys the smallest cake they have, a mocha crème. She adds two tall candles and three short ones for San's age. Su-ae pays and points at San, telling the cashier wearing the yellow-and-blue-striped apron, "It's this girl's birthday today."

"Really? Happy birthday!"

Shy at being congratulated by a stranger, San stands next to the air conditioner.

Su-ae hands over the cake, saying, "Share it with your friend, light the candles and everything! You've got to have cake on your birthday!" and returns to the flower shop. Her back obscures the sign for the Sapporo Udon House. Holding the cake box in one hand, San stands there until Su-ae's white calves are obscured by the blue buckets out on the street.

Even at eight in the evening, there's still a little sunlight left.

White, unladen clouds float in the evening sky; maybe they were left over from the squalls that had passed earlier that day. Thanks to the rain, the pavement has cooled and the evening is eminently walkable.

San walks until she happens to pass an Italian restaurant called Pomodoro.

Patrons line up outside for their turn at the spaghetti. San had thought there would be fewer people later and had been thinking of having dinner there. During lunch, the line at Pomodoro spills out into the street. San doesn't hate spaghetti but doesn't love it enough to get in line, so she's never eaten at Pomodoro before. From time to time, Su-ae would get in line to have seafood bolognese. Sometimes, she brings back garlic bread in a white paper bag. She never fails to mention how the chef at Pomodoro used to cook Italian food at Shilla Hotel. Whenever she does this, Su-ae seems like a parrot repeating a learned phrase. Su-ae says, This is really good, and her expression is serious as she hands over the garlic bread. She tells San that the spaghetti at Pomodoro is incomparably better than the spaghetti anywhere else. The thing that bothers me though, she admits, is they charge for the garlic bread when other places offer it for free. But when I taste it, I have to admit it's worth paying for. Su-ae never forgets to present that last bit of generosity.

San pauses in front of a vendor selling hairpins and necklaces and rings. It's difficult choosing one thing out of the many on display. After picking up and putting down various hairbands, she picks one with sparkling studs and holds it up to her neat, long hair. Soon, the hairband glitters in San's hair.

Having told Su-ae she was going to meet a friend and then having given up on dinner at Pomodoro, San now really has nowhere to go. She takes a few steps then pauses, another few steps, looks around, then turns toward the flower shop and stands there for a moment as if she's waiting for someone. She manages to make it to the foreign language cram school before stopping again. Then, she starts traveling down the street that has a bento box place, a stationery store, a framer's, a music shop with its display window full of violins, and a barbecue restaurant. She heads for Koryo Supermarket but then makes a full circle and walks toward the Sejong Arts Center's fountain on the other side. After resting on a bench in view of the fountain, she climbs up the steps leading to Gwanghwamun Plaza, walks past the cafés, arrives at the bus stop, and stands still again. She looks down at her toes peeping out of her sandals.

What could she be thinking?

She turns back toward the steps of the Sejong Arts Center and begins to walk.

The steps are decorated like a rural vegetable patch. Cement slabs hide underneath sponge gourds and kabochas pushing up through deep green leaves. A little farther off is a grove of long, tall reeds. There San stands in her droplet-patterned sundress. Blankly, she's climbed up all the steps that run through the vegetable patch installation. To her right is a café called Culture Love and a wall with copper panels engraved with the words of famous poets. Beyond the fountain and garden are skyscrapers.

She walks toward the copper panels.

Cake box in hand, she gazes over the words. She doesn't read the poems but turns around as if to walk back down the steps but then comes back to the poetry, and then turns again. In a thatched gazebo temporarily installed on the steps, a group of uniformed high school girls burst into giggles. San hesitates before coming down to the gazebo herself and sits down, stretching her legs. Balancing the cake box on her knees, she stares out into the darkening street. Her eyes are not fixed on one spot but move here and there. There is a large video screen on the side of a skyscraper. Its light makes the fake patch of real vegetables change color. Her gaze, having briefly paused on the screen, moves over to the Korea Telecom building and then stops at the street. Rush hour traffic has practically turned it into a parking lot. Buses, taxis, and cars have come to a complete halt.

She sits in the middle of the city in guarded silence.

Into her silence intrudes the light from the screen, the sound of a ringing cell phone, the prattle of a young man's sneakers as he runs down the steps. Thinking of something, she moves the cake box and rummages through her plastic bag. She finds the business card dropped by the man who had come out of the recreation office, and she holds it up to the city lights beginning to flash and whir. It had been on the stairway, and Su-ae had picked it up before tossing it once more. San had put it in her bag. The card wasn't printed at a shop. It had been cut from a larger piece of cardboard and written on by hand.

Three Years Later, it reads. *Three Years Later*, and a Daehak-ro address. She tilts her head. Three years later? Was it the name of a restaurant or a café? She examines the phone number written below the name and reads the words *Three Years Later* one more time. The longer she stares at it, the emptier her eyes become. She sits there in the gazebo until the vegetable patch lights are switched on. As darkness descends, the building lights grow brighter. Gazing down at the clogged traffic below her with an expression of unspeakable loneliness, San finally picks up the cake box and gets up.

She crosses the street through an underground tunnel, stands briefly at the bus stop in front of Kyobo Bookstore, and then walks toward Gwanghwamun Post Office before turning again at a crosswalk toward Mugwasu Bakery. She passes Jaeil Bank's headquarters, goes into another underground passage, and surfaces near the Bosingak bell pavilion. The street between the bell pavilion and Jongno Bookstore is filled with young people. Even when they try to avoid each other, they can't help bumping shoulders at the Pilot pen store or by the stalls of silk goods. Someone's knee brushes against her cake box, and her nose knocks against the shoulder of a man passing by.

There San is, unable to walk straight, weaving through the pedestrian traffic with her shoulders turned sideways. So many strangers. Briefly, she steps into the entrance of Jongno Bookstore to get out of the flow. Even there it's crowded with people looking at their watches or waiting for their dates to materialize. But at least they're not walking, which is a relief. The people on Jongno Street are mostly her age, youths wearing T-shirts and shorts. Their sandals are white or black or blue, and they nearly collide as they maneuver in the flow, their hair dyed yellow or red or brown as per the current trend. Those who do wear trousers wear them so loosely that they drag across the pavement. San stands there with her long black hair, in her sundress with the droplet pattern and prim collar, cake box in hand, sticking out in the crowd. Giving up, she rejoins the bumpy current and continues her walk. She turns onto a side street in order to avoid the crowds, and finds the vendors who normally line it are gone. Instead, there is a tree surrounded by a ring of benches, with people sitting in threes and fours, in front of a movie theater.

A stranger to every single person in the crowd, San finds herself blocking the sidewalk as people swerve to avoid her. Even if a carnival were to break out around her, the vacant expression on her face looks entrenched enough to persist. Is she trying to catch a movie? There she is, holding her cake box, scanning the posters. One cinema has three screens. A recent release is touted as having surpassed one million ticket sales. Perhaps this success is why the cinema, which normally shows three separate movies, is now showing this single one. She walks to the box office and looks at the showtimes. They're still selling tickets. Putting the cake box down, she rummages for the persimmon-dyed purse and unzips it. Packed among the coins are some folded ₩10,000 and ₩1,000 bills. She takes out a ₩10,000 bill, flattens it as best as she can, and slides it into the slot. A manicured hand takes the bill and returns to her a movie ticket and change. San folds the change into her coin purse, takes her ticket and cake box, and goes up to the theater. Screen 3 is on the third floor. People glance at her as she walks up the steps alone, carrying a cake. When she gets to the entrance of the theater, she sits down on a bench waiting for it to open. Her face fills with fatigue. Her swollen feet throb every time she stretches her legs and bends her knees. She sits there as the door of the theater opens and moviegoers crowd out. After a while, she gets up and goes inside to find her seat number. The movie theater is soon packed and she can smell popcorn and roasted squid. She sits flanked by pairs of lovers. She must've been tired; while she manages to stay awake for the ads and trailers, she nods off as soon as the movie begins, holding the cake box on her lap. A character on the screen says, *Sergeant Lee, how am I going to survive my service after your tour ends?* San tries to keep herself awake by opening her eyes wide, but consciousness proves too heavy a burden. She dozes off. Only when the ending credits roll and the audience begins to murmur and get up does she wake. Feeling bereft, she stares at the dark screen where the movie had played. Picking up the cake box, she goes out the cinema exit. Putting down the cake box on a bench outside, she massages her stiff neck before going to walk toward Jongno Street again.

It's as busy as ever.

Again her shoulders bump into other people, and the cars are still frozen in their traffic jams. She lingers for a while at a bus stop and gets on a bus that says Daehak-ro on the side. It takes more than thirty minutes to pass Jongno 4-ga toward Biwon. The distance normally traversed in fifteen minutes now takes fifty. San finally gets off at Daehak-ro on swollen legs. There isn't a breath of wind to break up the sweltering heat. She's now cradling the cake box in her arm like it's a pet dog. Her forehead and neck are slippery with sweat. Not to mention her armpits.

Is she searching for Three Years Later?

Now she's looking around the alleys of Daehak-ro. Occasionally she asks a passerby, Do you know where Three Years Later is? Her voice is so soft people have a hard time understanding her. Not knowing where to go, she wanders through the alleys, the flashing signs blinding her eyes. Next to a red brick wall, a young woman in a blue T-shirt and a young man wearing sandals are kissing passionately. The man's sandals stay on his feet solely by a single loop around the big toe. A little farther off is a young woman bending over and throwing up, while next to her yet another woman is ignoring her and swaying to the loud music coming from over the wall.

And what's that?

She walks toward what has caught her eye. A dog. There's a dog held inside a cage. Their eyes meet and the dog wags its tail. She puts down the cake box and looks at it. Where has she seen this dog before . . . Ah, she thinks, and smiles. Her ink bottle that wouldn't open, the man who helped her with it and then slammed the door in her face—this is the dog. The one that followed him down the stairs, the one that kept guard in front of the bathroom, waiting for him. She puts her hand through the wire bars and strokes its head. The dog lets her. Crouched down like that, the backs of her knees begin to sweat. Three Years Later. The place right next to the cage is Three Years Later. She hadn't been thinking about it at that moment, which makes her feel glad she found it. Silently saying goodbye to the dog, she picks up the cake box and goes to the café entrance. An aproned young server shouts, "Come inside," and then, "Are you alone?"

She nods. There she is, sitting down at the corner table she's been led to. A song with incomprehensible lyrics is playing.

It's a live café.

The music is not coming from speakers; it's coming from a stage mostly obscured by other patrons. Live music with no electronic amplification. The café is wider and deeper than it looks from the outside, with indirect yellow lighting scattered throughout. The stage is big enough for people to dance on, white and red light falling from above. Young people lean against the wall, swaying their heads. Some hold cans of beer as they move to the music, and there's also a long-haired man headbanging from where he sits. A girl clutching a handkerchief, also headbanging. Only after a long time does San realize that the man onstage, maniacally playing the guitar and singing a song with words she can't understand, is the dog owner. The man who opened her ink bottle for her, the one she bumped into in front of the recreation office. His movements are frenzied as people dance beneath the flashing lights. She glimpses him on one side of the stage, then in no time he's on the other side. She tries to get a good look at his face, getting up from her seat and turning her head, but it's useless. Giving up, she sits back in her chair for a while before getting up to go to the toilets. In the narrow hallway leading to the bathroom are four women shaking their bodies to the music. She struggles to get past them; a girl and a boy block the entrance and completely ignore her as they violently kiss. Farther in are four boys smoking cigarettes and staring at her. San gives up and goes back to her seat. There are other groups at the other tables with snacks and drinks. Quite a few couples as well, clinking beers together. San is back in her seat but the servers seem to have forgotten about her. They're so busy busing tables that they don't bother taking her order.

Perhaps she's hungry.

After sitting there for a time, she opens the cake box and slices the cake with a plastic knife from inside the box, eating the slices with her hands. She drops brown cinnamon powder on her dress. Her ears are about to burst from the resounding music. The people onstage hardly seem tired, dancing with the same frenetic energy. One of them wears a yellow helmet and spins on his head. Dancers surround him. As the man spins so fast he's able to lift his hands off the floor, people applaud.

Watching the dancers, San continues to eat the cake little by little, unaware the candles Su-ae had made sure to include are on the floor. Her mouth and nose are dusted with cinnamon powder. Youths with bleached blond hair and baggy trousers, youths surrounded by music but still wearing earphones and swaying to their own beat. Sitting there, San feels like she doesn't really exist. In the middle of intently eating her cake, she seems to suddenly think of something and closes the box and gets up. The servers, out of professional habit, call out goodbye as she leaves. The dog in the cage recognizes her and wags its tail. Crouching down once more, she takes a bit of cake and pushes it through the bars. San is uncertain whether or not the dog will eat anything sweet, but it laps up the morsel, and she gives it the rest. Passersby glance at the dog in the cage eating cake, with San huddled before it.

Now she's sitting on the subway.

She got on it after leaving Three Years Later and walking toward Jongno 5-ga, no longer carrying a cake box. Maybe she left it by the cage, because she's only carrying her transparent bag. Her gaze falls briefly on the drunk girl sitting across from her, nodding off with half-lidded eyes. Next to her, a group suddenly bursts into laughter over a funny story. Their faces are flushed red from drinking. The sleeping girl's skirt is riding up her knees, which makes San close her legs tighter. The droplets crease in her lap. There's a couple by the door; the male is vomiting while the female, with a pained expression, is holding on to his waist. A man with his head buried in a newspaper tosses the paper aside. Another man next to him takes it up. San, who had been watching the sleeping girl, slowly closes her tired, bloodshot eyes.

Her ears fill with the clunking of the subway car.

A face appears in her memory and she pushes it aside. San sees her mother, who would hold her head high in a crowd; other people would misunderstand, see her elegant gaze and assume that they were being pitied. Seeing her mother find love again and become an ordinary middle-aged wife hadn't been so bad, San thinks. Just like her childhood memories of tops spun on icy ponds, white kites flown on hills, the numerous big and little nickel-silver bowls they used back then—her vision of her mother has scattered. The fragments that remain float about in her mind like old relics. Her forehead, a cheek, the scent of her hair, her fingers, the scar underneath her knee, the little mole on her scalp near the whorl of her roots, these were all memories San would lose one day as well. San thinks now that her mother's delicate eyes could be said to be arresting. She never fit in with her surroundings, but her beautiful eyes made any clothes look as if they were made for her.

San's eyelids keep closing like an encroaching wave during an incoming tide; her mind is full of the plants she left behind some hours ago in the flower shop. The philodendrons that need occasional spritzing to ward off aphids, the monsteras with their giant leaves resembling ripped umbrellas, the winglike shape of the grass-green sago palms, the rubber figs that bled white when wounded in the stem, the lady palm that had been overwatered and needed to be repotted. Envisioning these trembling plants makes her eyes open. Drunk passengers stumble toward the train exits. A young female student wearing tight jeans stands conversing with a young male student, posed like they're going to begin dancing at any moment.

To determine where she is, she walks to one of the doors and looks up at the subway map. She's at Jongno 3-ga Station. Maybe she could get off here to catch a bus, but a sudden memory of the frozen traffic on Jongno Street stops her. As she transfers to Line 5 from the Jongno 3-ga Station and takes the new train over one more stop to Gwanghwamun Station, she hears in her ears the sound—*hu hu*—of the lady palm's roots she replanted earlier today. The sound is unbearable.

Like someone late for an appointment, she keeps looking at her watch as she leans against a pole next to the subway door. The shuttered flower shop is sure to be pitch-black inside. She's plagued with the thought of all those trapped plants lost in that darkness. Getting off at Gwanghwamun Station, San quickly makes her way through the underground tunnels and up the stairs leading outside. Her steps are purposeful as she walks through the streets. It's almost midnight. The fountain has been turned off. There's a couple on the bench, a man stretched out with his head cradled in a woman's lap. The woman strokes the man's hair. All people of the night, out despite the late hour. The glimmer from the streetlamps spills over them. San sees the soft yellow illuminating the Sejong Arts Center and quickens her pace. She crosses the empty parking lot and walks past a barrier with yellow-and-black caution stripes. Paris Baguette and the flower shop have their shutters down, but the Sapporo Udon House and the kimbap place are still open. Underneath one of the trees lining the street, next to a stack of black trash bags, a middle-aged man keeps shouting, "That's not it, that's not it."

San reaches the flower shop.

Only then does she discover that there has been a café on the second floor of the building all this time. San stares for a long time at the letters spelling out "Autumn" on its sign. The sound of guitars and singing floats out from its windows. She raises the shutters and unlocks the flower shop door. A stray cat darts for the trash bags. Inside the shop, San slowly calms herself down. Because they bring in all the outdoor plants at night, the inside of the shop is crowded. Carefully making her way through the shop's interior, she finds the switch on the wall and floods the darkness with light. She goes up to the repotted lady palm and crouches down. Water has seeped out from underneath the pot. As if to listen to its breathing, she leans over and places her ear close to the plant, and the lady palm's leaves brush her cheek like green fingers.

San, who turned twenty-three years old today.

She was led here by her own two feet, to care for the plants in the middle of the night. Her movements are shrouded in silence. It passes midnight. She repots some ivy into hanging gourds. It is now 1:00 a.m. She carefully plucks blackened leaves. The time passes 2:00 a.m. She trims branches that have gone leggy, long stems with too few leaves. She inserts supporting rods for vines to climb. She is so intent on wiping every single leaf of the white-striped spider plants that she's unaware of the taxi pulling up. Nor does she see Su-ae getting out of said taxi and peering into the windows of the shop before coming inside. When she realizes someone is with her, San shouts in surprise—her surprise is so great that her face pales for a moment.

Su-ae laughs.

San says, "What . . . What are you doing here?"

"I waited and waited for you to come home!"

"I thought you were a ghost."

"She said, looking like a ghost."

"What?"

Su-ae keeps laughing.

"You knew I was here?"

"Yup."

"How?"

"I used to be like that."

"Be like what?"

Su-ae's only answer is to smile.

"So that night you didn't come in, you were here doing this?"

"No, I didn't come to work like some ghost in the middle of the night. I just sat here. By the way, a letter came for you. Who's Lee Mirae?"

Su-ae hands over an envelope. San takes it from her and just stands there until Su-ae asks, "Aren't you going to open it?" before bringing over a pair of shears and snipping the letter open for her. San takes it to a clutch of weeping figs and sago palm trees.

Dear San,

I wonder if you'll get this letter on your birthday.

It crossed my mind for the first time today that you might never come to see me. I know I have no right to ask you anything. Knowing all too well what little I've done for you as a mother, I'm as disgusted as anyone else would be of me asking you this now.

I left you as a child and came back with only this disease to show for it. He's still alive, and I was his family when I was healthy, but now that I am sick I'm a stranger to him. Who am I to blame for this. Of course, it is firstly my fault for not trying to stand on my own two feet, and secondly my fault for not demanding he make our marriage official. How could I have known he would turn me out sick and poor. I want to fight, but now my own body fights against me.

How pitiful my life has become. And how shameless I am in looking for you. To have thought you would be here waiting for me if I ever returned. I learned of your address after a year of searching. If I were a real mother I would've come to visit you as soon as I'd learned it. But now I am too weak to do even that.

There is so much pain now.

Each day is like a rock that rolls down a hill and hits my

face. Every moment, I endure overwhelming pain.
Oh, San.
Please come see your mother one last time.
See the mother who left you behind, what a state she's in.
And San.
Please.
Please.
Euthanize me, for my sake.

San is so surprised she crumples the letter in her fist. Heat spreads across her face and her heart beats fast. The sound makes Su-ae look up. San, as if steeling herself for a violent confrontation, uncrumples the letter and reads on.

Forgive your mother for only having you to ask.
Please don't leave me here to suffer.
If you don't come, if you don't euthanize me, then I shall have to bear this pain alone until I die. And no one will know I have passed for over a day, or days, or a week.

San can read no more and stuffs the letter back in the envelope. Leaving the weeping figs and sago palms, she comes back to Su-ae. She doesn't answer when Su-ae asks what the letter was about. San thinks she needs to get rid of the previous letter, the letter on the kitchen shelf. In the eerie silence, Su-ae tries to lighten the mood by tossing a bunch of yellowed, bug-bitten ivy leaves at San's face, and tickles San's neck with one of the snipped-off leggy branches. They look at each other for a moment and burst into laughter at the same time.

Under the bright lights, the colorful flowers each showcase their distinct, vivid colors. On other nights the plants would've slumbered in the darkness of the shuttered shop, but tonight they wake up one by one to surround the two young women in an atmosphere of friendly complicity. The shop's lights have bled onto the street and their section of the block is as bright as day. In that brightness, as dawn begins to break, San and Su-ae sit smiling among the layers and layers of plants and flowers. San's gaze, which had been so empty as she wandered, has settled into a look of contentment. A drunk, having woken up on one of the fountain benches, happens to pass and peers inside the glass, and locks eyes with the young women inside. Perhaps their smiles are uncanny; he shakes his head as if he's seen a ghost and hurries off, all but running away. He looks back for a moment, but then shakes his head again, and walks faster. Maybe, when day finally arrives, the drunk will spread a rumor. A rumor that during the night, he came upon two ghosts in the city of Seoul.

So These Are Violets?

The monsoon season is upon them, and the intermittent rains begin.

The skies would be clear until 11:50 a.m., but then, as if suddenly remembering a chore, they would hastily cloud over and start pouring rain. The rain would pause for a brief spell but return in spurts, repeating this cycle three or four times. These days, San goes to the swimming pool with Su-ae at dawn. The day after San turned twenty-three was the first time Su-ae had dragged San to the pool, running from the Gwanghwamun flower shop at dawn back to the long room in Samcheong-dong, grabbing for San a spare swimsuit with blue stripes and an extra white cap. *But I don't want to go,* said San before Su-ae successfully cajoled her into joining her "just this once." Su-ae bought San a set of black goggles at the entrance where they sold tickets. She assured San she would teach her how to breathe and stroke and kick. And that if you knew how to do those three things, the crawl was easy. As San took off her clothes in the changing room and showered, she thought, Just this once. Really, just this once.

At dawn, the pool was filled with children who had signed up for summer vacation classes. A coach taught a chattering herd of children how to kick. In the lanes, advanced swimmers diligently moved back and forth. Their eyes hidden behind their goggles and hands outstretched as they sped through the water, they seemed incredibly active to San. When San entered the water, it revived a longing in her heart and she suddenly felt anxious. To hide her anxiety, she closed her eyes and listened to the gentle lapping of the water against her body. *Hey San*, Su-ae said as she splashed her— and a tremor passed through San. Slowly, she sank down, the gentle water covering her face and head, the water undulating around her. She stared down at the checkerboard pattern of the swimming pool floor. A minute passed. Su-ae was the one who was surprised; when San wouldn't come up for air, she called for her. *Are you all right?* As if that were the signal, San slowly raised her head and launched into a crawl, stroking the water and maintaining proper distance with the other swimmers. When she came back from swimming a lap of thirty meters, Su-ae was waiting for her at the edge of the pool. *Look at you! You're a better swimmer than I am!*

Once the storms pass, the trees on the avenue and inside the flower shop take on a deeper shade of emerald. More people came in to buy plants when it rained. They were mostly men. Men buying red roses on rainy days. Some men bought a single rose, others thirty-two blossoms. On rainy days, San and Su-ae would go to Samcheong Park to fill up a container with mountain spring water. Even on weekdays the springs bustled with lines of people, some-times until ten at night or even eleven. People would line up their bottles, each a different color and shape, and go for a walk in the park while they waited. Several times the two of them had gone out after dinner, but they had never succeeded in collecting any water.

Then one night, when the rain ceased only around 10:00 p.m. and the resulting humidity at midnight had made sleep impossi-ble, Su-ae suggested they go to the spring. They found the park completely devoid of people. Anyone gathering water would usually have to stretch the gourd deep down to scoop it up, but that night, the spring overflowed. When the rim of the gourd touched water

immediately, Su-ae exclaimed, *Oh my! It's filled up.* As if quench-
ing a long-held thirst, they drank as much as they liked and filled
their bottles to the brim. Su-ae, reluctant to leave so much water
behind, asked San to pour some over her neck so she could cool
down. The park was covered in water after the rain. San could
almost hear the moss on the rocks sucking in the moisture. Great
tangles of climbing vegetation had also drunk their fill, their leaves
richly colored. Despite the streetlamps, San accidentally stepped
into a deep puddle that came up to her ankle. They ran barefoot
over the dewy grass. Su-ae shook a tree full of raindrops over San's
head and cackled gleefully.

One Friday afternoon, a group of young women descends on the
flower shop like a squall, reserving bouquets and corsages. There
is to be a wedding at 2:00 p.m. that Saturday, so they will come
in at noon for the flowers. The women brush raindrops out of
their hair and approach the flowers exclaiming, Wow, these are so
gorgeous. San only listens as Su-ae asks about the bride's appearance and dress.

"Well, she's short. And she's put on some weight."

This last part is said with emphasis, and they all giggle.

"Look, she hasn't put on some weight, she's . . . in a hurry to
get married."

"Shh, you're supposed to keep that a secret!"

"Her parents don't know, apparently."

"Don't you think they're only pretending they don't know? I
mean, it makes it easier for everyone."

The young women laugh again.

"I guess that's true. How could they not know, when their children are getting married in the middle of summer?"

The bride is apparently the first of their friends to tie the knot
while pregnant. Su-ae recommends white roses but the young
women choose lilies, saying they are the bride's favorite.

"What if it rains?"

"We'll just have to hope it doesn't."

"It's good luck to rain on your wedding day!"

"That Myeong-hye. Does she really need more good luck? I mean, have you seen her new stereo system? Her mother-in-law-to-be bought it for her as a wedding present. It doesn't look like much, right? But it's the price of my key money!"

"Are you jealous?"

"How could I not be? What makes her better than any of us? Did she get better grades? Does she sing better? Is she better at sports? The only thing she's good at is plucking her eyebrows and penciling on a new pair."

"Oh, you didn't know? That's what she's definitely better at. Apparently, the groom fell in love with her because of her eyebrows."

"Really? If I knew that, I would've plucked mine a long time ago and practiced penciling them on every day."

"Myeong-hye would've loved to hear all this. Who knew you were such a serious rival? But before you could even issue a formal challenge, you were KO'd by her eyebrows."

The young women who descended like a squall leave behind a slew of raindrops and jokes and laughter. Su-ae had promised them a pretty crescent-moon bouquet, saying the shape suited shorter brides well. Once the bouquet had been decided, there was a flurry of conflicting opinions on what flower to use in the corsages. One friend liked roses, and another recommended carnations. In the end, they went with neither roses nor carnations but irises. Tapping the yellow stamens of the lilies chosen for the bride, one friend declared: I'm going to be the one who catches this bouquet.

After they have gone, San looks for a long time at the lilies they fondled. She stares until the white of the petals pierces back into her eyes, losing all sense of distance, leaving her feeling empty inside. Whenever this happened, she would close her eyes. Trying to overcome the lethargy that felt like she was falling into a hollow of white.

Almost as soon as Su-ae leaves for the wholesaler to buy some pots, a call comes in from the Gupabal farm. The voice on the line belongs to the young man on the farm. He says the flower shop owner is asking whether she has adjusted to her work. Never having been asked such a question, she ends up being a little short, saying, "Please tell him I'm learning as much as I can." Ever since Su-ae came back from her vacation, San has not seen the owner. Su-ae is usually the one to answer the phone, leaving San very little occasion to make conversation like this.

The owner seems to have left the shop completely in Su-ae's care.

It's understandable, as Su-ae is more than capable of running things. She's practically the owner herself. The young man says the owner wants to talk to Su-ae. When San says Su-ae has gone to the wholesaler, some serious, silent discussion seems to happen on the other end. Some moments later, the young man asks her if there are enough violets in the shop. San glances at some nearby violets and says they have several pots. He tells her that a photographer is going to arrive shortly and she should help him with his work. That a magazine they have ties to needs photographs of violets.

Another squall passes.

Raindrops stippling his hair, the photographer in question enters the flower shop.

The camera bag gives him away. His entrance fills the quiet shop with the smell of rain mingling with the scent of flowers. As soon as the man says, "Look at this rain," the sky is suddenly clear and blue as if it has never rained at all.

Handing him a towel to dab off the raindrops, San tells him the owner called ahead, and the man apologizes for being a nuisance. Not knowing precisely how he is going to be a nuisance, San watches the man's movements as he flicks the water from his hair and takes out his camera and adjusts the aperture.

He fiddles with his camera for a long time.

San picked out the wilted red roses from the buckets this morning, and the floor is littered with petals. Her mind wanders as she waits for the man to ask for her help, and she regards the scattered petals. Apparently finished, the man says, "Wait," and has her stand there with her downturned gaze as he presses the shutter. She looks up, puzzled, and the man only says, "Once more just like before," asking her to look down at the wilted petals on the floor, and presses the shutter again. But taking her picture seems to be a sudden whim, not the work she has been told to help him with.

"Which ones are the violets?" the man asks as he stops adjusting his lens at her face.

San chooses a pot with three or four blossoms and brings it out, and the man frowns.

"So these are violets?"

His voice is loud and incredulous, as if violets are supposed to be something else and she has brought out the wrong thing. To help him take photos, San moves some other pots to make room for the plant that has produced delicate purple flowers.

The man takes pictures of the violets on the shelf.

Violets. They bloom everywhere, making them seem more like weeds than proper flowers. San takes a closer look at them. Their little green leaves are small, their purple blossoms tiny. Before she came to the flower shop, she knew them as swallow flowers. Memories of entangling two swallow flower stems together and pulling them apart—one side was bound to snap. Whoever's stem didn't was the winner. She forgot what the prizes were, but she'd played the game many times. They did it with broadleaf plantains; they did it with foxtails. The man keeps pressing the shutter and mumbling something discontentedly.

"What's so pretty about these flowers? Such nonsense."

His disappointment is so palpable, it makes her apologetic. "Would you like to see them in some other color?"

"You have them in colors other than purple?"

"We have many. White, yellow, pink, even multicolored."

"Multicolored?"

"Light pink mixed with purple."

San gathers an array of colors from around the shop. Examining the other colors does nothing for his scowl.

"What's so pretty about these flowers," he mutters, and suddenly makes eye contact with San.

"Do you like these flowers too, miss? They did a survey of female elementary school teachers and violets came out on top; can you believe it? Did they even know what violets look like? I bet they voted for them because of the name. How are we going to make a cover out of this flower? They're not going to blame the flower; they're going to blame me!"

As if finding this prospect unbearable, he keeps muttering away as he snaps at the purple violets, the yellow violets, and even the back of the violets. The quiet, gentle violets endure the man's complaints and the flashes from his camera. Unsatisfied, the man takes his hand off his camera and lifts up the pot, examining it from this angle and that angle. Struck by an idea, he takes the pot out of the shop. Outside the sun has already dried up the street. The man considers the slender calla lilies, baby's breath, and China pinks displayed on the pavement. He looks like he wants to photograph those instead of the violets.

He says to San, "Sorry, but could you move those violets out here?"

He is pointing specifically to a spot on the sidewalk. Still unsatisfied, he brings out a wooden folding chair from somewhere inside the shop and places the pot on it. Staring at the violets exposed to bright sunlight makes San's eyes water; she blinks. Placing them outdoors doesn't do much for their plainness. Violets also detest bright light. The man, back to taking photos, still glowers in discontent. Passersby stop and stare at him focusing on the violets. Their expressions seem to ask, Why is he so interested in those pathetic flowers?

"Wait, can you stand there?" The man has his lens trained at her again.

Before she knows it, she's trapped inside his viewfinder along with the yellow and purple and light pink of the flowers. Snapping several shots from her profile and front, he tells her to look down. As he shoots away at her, his frown disappears. There are beads of sweat gathered on his forehead from the effort.

"Please stop," San says waving her hand at him.

But when the man's lens refuses to turn away, she hides behind some plants. Shrugging, the man returns his attention to the violets. The scowl that had disappeared while he was taking her picture is back.

San goes back inside to bring out a cup of cold water. Aside from that, there's nothing else to help him with.

"Hey darling, if you want those photos I took of you, call me at this number."

Taking three rolls of film still hadn't been enough to erase his disappointed frown. The card he holds out features the title *Flower World* in gold embossed letters along with the man's name and phone number. Darling. All she can do is look up at this photographer who used the word "darling" without missing a beat. Once he's packed his camera, the man takes out a magazine as if getting rid of some cumbersome garbage and tosses it on the steel table. The half-folded magazine blooms to lie almost completely flat.

After the man leaves with his frown and his photos, San takes a moment to read the name stamped on his business card before dropping it in a box with other customers' cards.

Of course! That was all it was!

San's first meeting with this man was as bland and quiet as this. He would later whip her empty heart into a certain frenzy. But that first time, he barely made an impression, much less aroused her attraction. His clothes, his height, the look in his eyes, his shoes, his silhouette. None of this drew her interest. Just like he had tossed the magazine, she, too, tossed his business card. His card became lost in the crowd. How different this meaningless, colorless meeting was to the one on the day she was hired, when she first met Choi. She remembers Choi very clearly, remembers guardedly shrinking back from him. His cropped haircut like an athlete's, the clean razor-shaved edges, the shining black shoes. The tiny wrinkles in the corners of his eyes, his grinning mouth, and the white ramie cloth of his shirt.

A Delicate Gaze

It's the day the ficus bonsai trees arrive from Indonesia. The two young women go swimming at dawn, then eat their breakfast, change, and leave directly for the farm. In the shop, trapped behind the shutters, the plants and flowers will spend the day without light. Six thousand trees are scheduled to come in that day, many more than the workers at the farm can handle. That's what Su-ae's uncle, speaking through the young man, told them over the phone.

White clouds float by.

Is it because of the summer sky? Or their hats? The two women on the bus look more like they're going on a picnic. San gazes out the window next to Su-ae, who sits with her eyes closed. Usually, Su-ae would return from the pool to the apartment and bury her tired face in her pillow for about fifteen minutes. There hadn't been time to do so that day.

The bus passes Gupabal Crossway and runs toward Tongil-ro Highway.

A sign reads Tongil-ro, Munsan, Ilsan as the bus crosses the border between Seoul and Gyeonggi Province. The numerous signs for open-air markets, bus stops, subway stations, and restaurants peter out as they enter Gyeonggi Province. The bus doesn't go up the ramp onto the highway but instead turns left into one of the "new towns" surrounding Seoul.

A faraway mountain ridge. Above it, the pure white clouds of a clear summer morning. They're not so far from the city but it's already much more peaceful. Sprawled beneath the mountains and clouds are signs for the large barbecue restaurants common in this area. San occasionally jerks in her seat whenever the bus driver hits the brakes. Su-ae also rocks forward.

There are fewer buildings or people now. There's the occasional sign pointing to driving schools, auto repair shops, or gas stations. Then, as if in a dream, they pass a sudden long stretch of flower shops. Yellow chrysanthemums stand out in front, ready to bow and usher in incoming customers. As the flower shops recede into the distance, San twists her head to watch. They pass houses, followed by wild mountain forests. The bus runs over the asphalt lettering that spells out the name of the new town, and passes about four crosswalks and then a sign for the Sangleung-dong Administrative Office. She sees other signs, mostly for farms: Hanyang Farm, Namdo Farm, Daehan Farm.

San and Su-ae get off the bus and walk down in the direction of the Sangleung-dong office.

The air is different here. There is a freshness San and Su-ae can only get on their occasional evening visits to Samcheong Park. As they continue walking, they pass a stone signpost with the name "Dongmaruteu" engraved on it; beyond it are greenhouses built of clear plastic. It's hard to imagine anyone living here, but when they finally come upon a road just wide enough for a car, San and Su-ae pass houses, a stream, and, in the distance, an elementary school. Was class in session? The playground is empty. They walk by a house with a big ginkgo tree in the yard. At a little general store, Su-ae buys a box of Bacchus energy drinks.

"They sell Bacchus at a general store?"

"They do here. Don't they sell them in other places?"

"I don't know. I mean, I thought only pharmacies sold them."

"Huyaya and Nadang and Henny like Bacchus."

"Huyaya? Nadang?"

"They work on the farm. They're Indonesians."

The two women pass a house with neatly trimmed hedges. There's a collie tied to a post. The dog has white, black, and yellow mixed into its fur. Despite the two strangers, it doesn't bark. If anything, it thumps its tail in hopeful greeting; it must be lonely.

Not all the greenhouses grow flowers. Some grow lush lettuce and a variety of organic vegetables. In fact, San notices, greenhouses with blooming flowers seem quite rare.

"Henny! Huyaya!"

Su-ae calls out to the Indonesians chatting at the farm's entrance. A suntanned man with curly hair and a woman, her head covered with a towel, turn toward Su-ae. Immediately, the woman runs to Su-ae and gathers her in a hug. Her brown eyes are clear and kind. This is Henny, and Su-ae holds out the box of Bacchus to her.

"Your favorite, Henny!"

An Indonesian woman who likes Bacchus.

San's eyes grow wide as she steps onto the farm.

It really isn't what she thought it would be. She had imagined the farm to be a big lawn filled with trees and flowers, but the actual farm looks about two or three thousand pyeong wide. There are multiple greenhouses made of plastic, some covered with shading nets. In between the greenhouses are countless trees. Farther along there's a grassy riverbank where the ficus bonsai stand in uniform rank, their luscious leaves spread out to the sun. Whenever the wind blows through them, the rippling green makes San stare. It's like the leaves are sighing in unison, *Ahhh—*. How long had it taken for these plants to grow from seed inside the greenhouses?

Still staring, San follows Su-ae inside one of the greenhouses.

This greenhouse serves as the farm's office. Su-ae explains that, due to zoning ordinances, no permanent buildings are allowed within Seoul's designated Green Belt. Whenever a new building is erected, the city sends a helicopter to photograph it. Her uncle lives in a greenhouse as well. Despite being covered in plastic, Su-ae says it's still as sturdy and cozy as any house made of brick.

The farm owner's eyes light up as he greets them.

He is in complete and utter farmer's mode.

It's a very different look from when San saw him in the flower shop. Now, he wears a white shirt, a straw hat, and roomy trousers rolled up to his knees. His calves are as dark as Henny's face. His legs look firm and muscled, healthy, from walking constantly, day and night. Like the lush ficus ruffling their green leaves by the riverbank.

Inside the greenhouse there is a desk with a fax machine, a computer, and other equipment. Scattered about are a book titled *Flowers in Goyang* and other volumes on trees and flowers. On a wall is a shelf filled with "character pots" that have celebrity caricatures drawn on them, and a poster next to the shelf says, *See the Stars and Grow Some Flowers: Character Pots! Celebrities Fresh from Your Own Pot!* Seeing San take a closer look, Su-ae asks, "So what do you think, are we going to be rich or what?"

When San looks at her askance, Su-ae says, "Uncle has a patent out on that; he says if it does well, we'll be rolling in it!" She laughs.

"Uncle is hilarious. You know how even Pokémon have their own brand of pastries?"

Pokémon pastries?

"Kids buy them for the stickers they come with, not for the bread. Some of them take out the sticker and throw the bread away. Uncle got his idea from that. Something about how collecting the pots of your favorite celebrity caricatures and raising plants would be good for kids. If the plant dies, you can still use the pot for your pens or letters or other junk, according to him. What do you think? Will kids go for it?"

"Well . . ."

"That's definitely not the response he's going for. It has to work! We have to pay the celebrities to be caricatures and everything."

"What are they made of?"

"Marble."

Then Su-ae mumbles "Marble . . ." again as she takes another good look at the pots. "Hey Uncle, I think you can make them out of clay, too."

The farm owner nods. Then, perhaps thinking his response inadequate, he takes out his notepad and writes, *Good idea*, and shows Su-ae.

"And if you make them here, I don't think you'll even cover the labor costs."

Su-ae goes and sits down next to him. While he can understand her speech, she conducts the rest of the conversation through his notepad. The farm owner writes that he's thinking of having the pots manufactured in China or Indonesia. That he might set up a factory overseas. That Huyaya's little brother had worked on the farm for two years before returning to Indonesia and he wanted to come back, that he would probably do a good job overseeing the character pot production. Su-ae mentions that Huyaya's brother bought two taxis back home in Indonesia. Her uncle answers that he hires them out and doesn't drive them himself, that he'll be more than able to manage the project.

When talking to the farm owner like this, Su-ae seems like an ordinary adult. To San, the two don't look like a niece and uncle but business partners. The character pots already fill up the display, ready for business to start tomorrow if need be. There are also pots shaped like boots, letterboxes, and mugs, all around the same size—suitable for planting flowers, but they'd need to be bigger for most plants.

The farm owner writes, *The containers will be arriving soon. Show Miss Oh the place until then, it's her first time here.*

Su-ae writes, *I was about to,* and puts down the pen.

The two women walk outside and are accosted by sunlight. Su-ae looks more carefree than San's ever seen her. Su-ae bends over, duck butt and all, to inspect plants or pick up stray rocks or grab a handful of palm mulch to sniff, acting like someone who has come home.

Next to Su-ae or following a step behind, San thinks about what Su-ae said in the flower shop. The words come back before scattering away again: *I did not want to give her the satisfaction of seeing me live a good life. I wanted to ruin what life I had left.* Su-ae on the farm has none of the vengeful vitriol of someone determined to ruin her own life. Mixed into the summer breeze is the smell of manure and earth.

"Smells terrible, right?" Su-ae wrinkles her nose, but she is smiling at the same time. "I didn't notice it when I lived here, but after I left, I missed the smell so much."

San walks with Su-ae.

"You know, when I was little, I'd play with the other kids outside until the sun set. All the moms calling in their children. Kids can play all day but that one sound will bring them home."

". . ."

"When I was away, this smell would call for me like mothers calling for their kids at sunset. I'd be fine one moment but just a whiff would make me long to come back here. Breaking my heart."

Maybe this is why Su-ae seems so at home here.

San changes the subject.

"How many pyeong is the farm?"

"The farms around here are about ten thousand pyeong, and Uncle owns about three thousand of it."

Three thousand pyeong. The magnitude is too much for San, who simply replies, "How prosperous your uncle must be."

The word "prosperous" makes Su-ae laugh.

"Only if they abolish the Green Belt policy. You see how close it is to Seoul. They'll put up apartments as soon as the Green Belt is gone."

"Then what happens to this farm?"

"It gets moved farther out into the countryside, I guess."

"Your uncle must want the Green Belt abolished."

"Not really. Uncle doesn't seem interested in any of that. No one interested in that kind of stuff would put this much effort into growing things. Or agonize over character pots. I mean, Uncle really loves working here."

"He owns all this land?"

"Yup."

"He must be rich still."

"He inherited it."

The farmer, who inherited all this land.

"He's lived here a long time. Uncle never dreamed of leaving it, ever."

There is lucky bamboo growing in one of the greenhouses.

Much of the shop's lucky bamboo is grown here. It's a popular choice. Even customers who come looking to buy flowers take one look at them and ask, What plant is this? Su-ae explains every time that they're auspicious bamboo, and having them in your home or office leads to good things. Just like Su-ae says, Koreans are particularly susceptible to superstitions surrounding flowers and plants; the inquirers often end up taking lucky bamboo with them. Sometimes they walk in with gloomy expressions, but seem to leave refreshed.

Toward the end of their tour, San and Su-ae enter a greenhouse growing striped dracaenas. Su-ae explains that the popularity they'd once enjoyed has moved on to lucky bamboo. These striped dracaenas were a side project of a long-time employee of her uncle.

"One second." Su-ae peeks into some greenhouses and darts inside one. Her head pops out again, her hand gesturing for San to come inside. "It's over here!"

Inside is a line of trees that have just started to sprout leaves. San gasps. It's so spacious. There's even a conveyor belt, flanked by chairs.

"Here they are! The papaya palms I told you about! You know, the two papaya seeds that got mixed in with the ficus and sprouted here."

The papaya trees stand by the entrance about a meter apart.

"They're still growing," Su-ae says proudly.

The still-growing trees are exactly the same height. They come up to San's waist. Long, like the legs of an adolescent boy. Along that length are green leaves. The twin trees even have the exact same number of leaves, seven each.

"So tropical plants can grow in Korea, too."

"Well, we're inside a greenhouse."

"What is your uncle going to do when they're bigger?"

"Plant them outside, of course."

"Wouldn't they mind the climate?"

"I don't know about palms. Other trees are grown inside here and we wait until they're strong before putting them out. The ones outside were all grown in the greenhouse. But this is the first time we've grown papaya palms. Not even Uncle knew what they were until they grew this much. He only realized it after the leaves began to sprout."

"..."

"It's amazing! Two seeds, growing into this. And they're all alone here, too. Side by side. Like friends, right?"

San doesn't know what to say.

"Shall we name them?"

"Name them what?"

"We can call this one Oh San, and that one Lee Su-ae."

Su-ae laughs, and San laughs along with her. Beyond the two papaya palms are dozens of ficus in pots, reaching their green leaves up to the sky.

From between the ficus slinks a gray cat.

Seeing the cat, Su-ae calls out, "Hi!," and waves at it. The cat ignores her, slowly walking toward them and settling down between the papaya trees. The cat has a white spot on its gray back and doesn't offer the slightest trace of friendliness; if anything, it's hostile. When San happens to catch its eye, its gaze is so contemptuous that it makes her feel unsettled. The contempt isn't only in the cat's eyes. It's also in a grimacing old wound that looks like stitches running down its cheek, twisting the cat's nose and mouth, making it look ready to strike and hiss at any moment.

On instinct, San steps away but then takes a closer look.

The white spotting isn't just on its back but also on its tail and tummy. Perhaps the cat is pregnant, because its tummy sags a little. It seems uncomfortable. It rises from its position and digs away at the soil before lying down once more. Its back is higher than most other cats and it has somehow folded its bulging stomach into the depression in its chest. Unlike when it was walking, the cat now seems shrunken and modest. Like the two women, it contemplates the ficus from the vantage point of the papayas. More like a friend of Su-ae's and San's than a cat. San watches, amused. She's about to say something when Su-ae shushes her, putting a finger to her mouth. It is obvious she does not want to disturb the cat.

They leave the greenhouse, carefully avoiding the cat, and Su-ae takes San toward the riverbank at the end of the farm. There, in an empty lot, are many fully grown ficus, shining and luscious and green in the sun. Whenever the wind blows, the thousands of leaves flip in one direction, and the sight dazzles San to the point where she must close her eyes. The sweat on her forehead evaporates.

Su-ae, walking on ahead, looks back. The gray cat with the white spots has left the greenhouse and is slowly trailing them.

"I think that cat has it out for you," whispers Su-ae.

"What?"

San looks behind her. The cat, matching its pace to theirs, maintains a precise distance behind the two.

"What do you mean, has it out for me?"

The riverbank is overgrown and verdant. There are babbling streams running on either side of an irrigation dike. Waterweeds line the bottom, and purple wildflowers quietly make their presence known through the mess of green. Su-ae glances covertly at the cat—nearly dragging its stomach as it leisurely follows them—before whispering in San's ear.

"Uncle hates cats. But that one arrived one day. No idea from where. It was just sleeping in one of the greenhouses. Hurt, with a torn ear. Uncle figured it was a feral cat and needed a place to stay for a little while and left it alone, but then it never went away. Its ear is all healed. Always underfoot, driving Uncle crazy. He really detests cats."

When the cat comes closer, she falls silent.

The cat doesn't come up to the top of the dike where the two women are. It simply lies down on the incline. Curling up, it regards them, silver in the summer sun. Su-ae sits down, stretching her legs. San sits down next to her. The cat and the women are in a stare-off.

"That cat is like that, you know."

"Like what?"

"It knows we're talking about it. That's why it's hanging around us and lying there."

San and Su-ae can see the whole farm from the riverbank. To the right, past a big road, is a farm with well-manicured trees grandly standing on display. That side of the road doesn't seem to be part of the Green Belt, because among the trees is a half-constructed house. In the haze, San can just about make out workers climbing what will be the roof.

Su-ae whispers in her ear again.

"Uncle once put that cat in a sack and went down Jayu-ro Highway past Ilsan, all the way to Reunification Hill. He dumped it under a bridge there. In the middle of the night. But four days later, the cat reappeared on the farm, limping."

San waits for Su-ae to continue.

"I've heard of Jindo dogs making their way back to their owners but have you ever heard of a cat doing it?"

"I don't know. I did hear somewhere that dogs attach themselves to people but cats attach themselves to places."

"Places? The party in question wasn't even born here!"

Party in question? The expression breaks the tension and San laughs.

"So it lives here now?"

"Yeah . . . I think Uncle feels guilty about going to such lengths to throw it away. Now he feeds it and he made a bed for it and everything. Isn't it the meanest-looking cat, though?"

"It's mean of you to say that about someone who's pregnant."

"Mean of me?" Su-ae incredulously asks in reply, adds a *Hmph!*, and then a laugh.

The cat gets up and walks away to a far corner where palm mulch is piled. Its head hangs so low it almost touches the ground.

"See? It knows when we're talking about it."

An old wound that looks like stitches.

San can't tear her eyes away. The cat looks determined to make it to the end of the world. How did it find its way back after being whisked away in a sack? A sudden rush of pity leaves her speechless. If it weren't for Su-ae, she would've run to it and caressed its scar. The cat, which had trusted in the solid ground, suddenly steps on some earth that gives way and stumbles, before heaving itself up again and walking away. Even when San can't see it anymore, her long gaze refuses to leave the smudge of gray and white.

The stream babbles.

In that moment, Su-ae playfully makes as if to push San into the water. San snaps out of her thoughts and jumps, launching to her feet shouting, "Stop that!" Her eyes blaze.

Overwhelmed by San's reaction, Su-ae looks up, her face asking, Are you all right?

The dark pupils of Su-ae's eyes as she stares at San. Embarrassed, San sits back down with some force, as if pushed down by her shoulders.

"It was just a joke. What's with that look you gave me?"

San is silent.

Below the dike, the leaves of the ficus rustle in one direction. There's a line of trucks coming down the twisting road where the two young women had traveled earlier. Four shipping containers, back-to-back, leaving a cloud of white dust in their wake.

"There goes our break. Come on, let's go back."

With some residual awkwardness, Su-ae makes her way down first. San looks down at the stream Su-ae had pretended to push her into a moment ago. It was because of the green shining ficus. And this water. When Su-ae had placed her hand on San's back, she had felt vertigo akin to being pushed off a cliff. San had lived through this scene before. And that was what had made her shout.

Su-ae leaves San behind on the dike and walks away.

San shakes off her uneasiness and gets up, calling for Su-ae, breaking into a run. Memory is an unannounced visitor. It lies crumpled in some corner of the body, then suddenly knocks on the door of reality and makes you scream. San finally catches up.

"Are you mad at me?"

When San takes Su-ae's arm, Su-ae half-heartedly shakes her off. San takes her arm again. Su-ae, conceding defeat, rolls her eyes and slaps San lightly on the back, grinning.

"Whenever you push me away, it really makes me rethink our friendship!"

San sighs deeply. Out of Su-ae's sight, she looks up at the floating clouds.

Back then, there was a minari field. An irrigation ditch where clear water flowed. A dike they dried their wet clothes on. A girl whose father would get drunk and crawl into a jar to sing. A small white back, and a green spot like a grass stain. Black pupils. Braided hair sitting on delicate shoulders. Thin cheeks splashed with water. Why did San think of that girl when Su-ae pushed her?

"Come on, let's go."

Shaking off the creeping memories, she unlinks their arms and takes Su-ae's hand instead, breaking into a run.

Each forty-foot container carries eleven hundred ficus trees, none of them with leaves, only trunks. Su-ae cautions San to treat them gently, so as not to injure them. Huyaya, Nadang, Su-ae, and San soon fall into a regular rhythm. Huyaya is inside the container passing the trees to Nadang, Su-ae, or San, who carry them into the greenhouses, careful not to damage the roots. When they've unloaded about half the trees, the young man who works on the farm, who had been away on some errand, pulls up behind the trucks and joins them.

Huyaya gets down from the container and the young man takes his place. San wonders if the others have mastered the art of communicating without words. Despite their silence they occasionally laugh in unison, and from time to time, Nadang goes to the farm owner to retrieve something without using any words. The tanned hands of the farm workers occasionally brush against San's as they pass the ficus to her. They have completely given themselves over to the flow of the task, so much so that San might as well just be another tree, albeit one with helping hands.

To San, the trees brought in from Indonesia seem to be no more than slightly thicker branches. She looks toward the irrigation stream where the mature trees stand shimmering under the summer sun. Cautiously, she strokes the mulch-covered root. How could it be that such green leaves would sprout from this bleak stick of wood?

Once the four thousand four hundred ficus have been offloaded, the trucks drive away in a cloud of dust once more.

The workers gather to eat naengmyun noodles at a picnic table by one of the greenhouses. They ordered two more bowls than there are workers; the farm owner wanted extra servings for whoever might want more. Chips of ice float in the clear beef broth. Nadang and Huyaya bring their bowls up to their lips and drink, ice chips and all. The sound of their gulps is a clear, delicious sound.

Nadang, who has dark eyes and thick eyebrows, drinks for longer than Huyaya. He finally lowers his bowl and exhales, looking as if he's cooled down at last, and smiles at San when their eyes happen to meet. San smiles back.

Too hot for anything else, Su-ae listlessly stirs her chopsticks in the leftover wisps of noodles. Beneath her straw hat, her forehead is drenched with sweat. She takes the farm owner's notepad, finds an empty spot, and writes: *You ordered a bunch of trees to arrive in the middle of summer?*

I didn't have enough, he writes back.

There are that many orders?

They're all people are looking for these days. Rubber figs, they're just second fiddle now.

Are they more popular than lucky bamboo?

Maybe not as much.

Su-ae nods and puts down the pen. The farm owner slips the notepad back into his pocket and, with his bowl still in front of him, puts a cigarette in his mouth and lights it. The blue flame of his lighter is nearly transparent in the sunlight. *Hu*— The farm owner, as he exhales smoke and glances about the farm, is sweating down to his earlobes.

Most of the work importing plants is done in the spring and fall; bringing in plants in the summer like this is rare. Trees imported in the spring would mature in the summer, as would those brought in during the fall through the winter. Apparently, these particular ficus trees had become an unexpected hit with the wholesalers and so more had been rushed in.

When Huyaya finishes his naengmyun, he gets up. Despite the farm owner gesturing to sit back down and take a break, Huyaya says he has to mix some more potting medium.

The farm owner announces he has somewhere to be and gets in his truck with the young man. Sitting on the passenger side, he takes out his notepad and writes to Su-ae. *Don't work too hard . . . Take the occasional nap . . . We don't need to do everything today.*

Sitting in the driver's seat, the young man dabs at the sweat on his forehead with a yellow towel. The truck kicks up dust as it leaves the farm. There's Huyaya, sweating as he mixes the potting medium. After the truck leaves, Nadang lies down on one of the picnic table benches, probably to nap. Summer floods the farm but there isn't a trace of wind. In the greenhouse used as a lounge, the two women lie down on a raised platform. All three wall-mounted fans are on, filling their ears with the sound of the whirring motors.

"Who made that?"

San looks up at a skylight, a square of blue. It's like looking into a well.

"Huyaya did."

"He must be clever with his hands."

"He really is. He can make anything. One time, he found a bicycle wheel from somewhere and made a wheelbarrow with it. That table is his handiwork."

San takes a look at where Su-ae is pointing. A plane of wood with four short legs. Unlacquered, which is why the nail marks are clear. It seems that there are talented tinkerers all over the world.

"But he has a sad story."

"What do you mean?"

"Before he came here, he had a wife and a baby who died in a fire. He's the only one to survive. But strangely enough, he's always kind and smiles a lot and works harder than everybody else."

Su-ae sits up and puts a cigarette in her mouth. She ignores San, who stares as Su-ae produces a lighter and clicks it on. The pack of cigarettes? The lighter? They seem familiar somehow.

"They're Uncle's. It looked so good when he was smoking just now that I filched them from his pocket."

San has never seen Su-ae smoke before; Su-ae inhales and exhales adroitly enough. With the cigarette between her fingers, Su-ae lies down again next to San.

"It still tastes great . . . Wanna puff?"

"I'll just get a headache again."

"You've tried it before?"

"Just once."

"You've got to get over the headache thing in the beginning. Everyone feels that way at first." Su-ae exhales another plume. "Eh. I guess it isn't something worth 'getting over' in order to do."

Despite her words, she hands over the cigarette once she's smoked half of it. There San is, placing it between her lips. She continues coughing after.

Su-ae's mumbles seem to come from somewhere far away. "I smoked three packs a day at one point. Then one day I just got sick of it. So I quit. I haven't smoked in a long time."

Ever since Su-ae had feigned pushing her into the stream, San had felt a heavy darkness in her chest. The whole time she was moving ficus trees, she had felt as if she were teetering on the edge of something. And here she was, Su-ae's cigarette between her lips. Her heartache and vertigo worsen, making her feel as if the sky is about to burst through the ceiling into the greenhouse.

"What do you think of Uncle?"

The sudden question makes San turn her head toward Su-ae.

"I think he's a good person."

"That's it?" Su-ae turns, facing herself away from San. ". . . I love him."

Her unexpected confession keeps San's gaze fixed on Su-ae's back.

"I've never met anyone more considerate toward others. He has no idea how much I love him. If he knew, he might kick me out. Poor Uncle. He doesn't know what a beautiful person he is, what a good air he has about him. This farm is his everything. I would want to be Uncle's voice if I could. But no . . . It's all just a dream."

Is that how it is? San hears Su-ae's voice like an echo from afar. She loves her uncle. That's why she would look so sad from time to time. Su-ae seems to have nodded off, and San tosses the cigarette butt underneath the raised platform.

All afternoon they shake the palm mulch off the ficus roots and plant the trees in pots with the medium mixed by Huyaya and move them to a greenhouse where Nadang and San water them. The potting medium is mostly made of granite soil, which drains well, and so the water drenches the roots and flows out the bottom of the pots. San, unused to the labor, is the only one who isn't fiercely efficient with her hands. With no one ordering them around or even much discussion, the other workers move as one. When the farm owner returns with the young man, their work reaches peak flow state. Despite this, planting six thousand ficus trees can't be done in one day. Summer days are long, but it would still take four days at least.

When the sun sets, San's cheeks are red from exertion. Nadang brings everyone misutgaru powder mixed in ice water. They each drink a bowlful. How delicious. San drinks an extra half bowlful.

When Su-ae and San are about to leave, the farm owner tells Su-ae to go see the bougainvillea. That it has flowered behind the middle greenhouse. Seeing Su-ae hesitate he adds, *You won't regret it.* He ushers the two women, wiping the sweat from his brow with the towel around his neck.

"Wow." Su-ae's eyes grow wide. "White flowers!"

The farm owner writes that he has grafted different flowers onto the plant. In the light of the setting sun, the bougainvillea glows. *Look,* writes the farm owner, *the yellow buds turn into yellow flowers and the white buds turn into white ones.* The two women stand before the bougainvillea. It's like seeing someone who had left to go far away but has finally returned. San and Su-ae admire the blooming yellow and white. Yellow and white are not the only colors; magenta is also in full bloom.

They walk back up the road from which they came.

"Isn't my uncle just like a little kid," remarks Su-ae as she winds an arm through San's. "He waited a long time for those flowers. It was his first time grafting on bougainvillea."

As soon as they leave the farm grounds, they see a local bus approach.

"Hey! That'll take us to Bulgwang-dong!"

Su-ae releases her arm and breaks into a run.

When I First Saw You

The women return to the closed flower shop.

They're dropping by because Su-ae left her wallet inside. On the bus back, Su-ae suggested they pick it up and have a nice dinner and some cold beer. Exhausted from working on the farm all day, San only wants to go back to the apartment, but she did hurt Su-ae's feelings earlier and so decides to humor her. Su-ae goes in to get her wallet, and San waits outside the half-shuttered shop. Only when Su-ae takes longer than usual does she enter; the lights are still off, and San switches them on as Su-ae searches in the dark. The air is still humid despite being closed in all day. There's a certain smell to it. It's the breath of trapped plants that haven't seen fresh air over the course of a day. The ficus trees on the farm drinking in sunlight next to a stream, their leaves rustling in the breeze—San raises the shutters, feeling sorry for the plants inside.

"You don't have to do that, we're leaving soon."

"I just wanted to let the air out a bit."

San opens the doors of the shop. Anything pooled or trapped, without exception, starts to smell. More so because things have their own smell. San sprinkles the dry floor with water. She half covers the hose's jet with her thumb to make the water fan out, drenching the dry windows, droplets splattering all over the glass.

Even when Su-ae says, "All right, let's go," San is refilling the water in the buckets that hold the cuttings. Giving up, Su-ae picks up a sprinkler and waters the pots and the herbs in the hanging planters. How much time has passed?

The two women finally close the shutters on the revived shop. Where do they go now? San and Su-ae drag their feet until they stop in front of Pomodoro. Maybe because of the late hour, Pomodoro looks a bit empty tonight. Normally, there would be a long line out the door, new patrons immediately filling tables as soon as they are vacated.

"Let's eat here."

Su-ae doesn't even give San a chance to hesitate, and strides into the restaurant. It's cool inside thanks to the air-conditioning. The fragrance of garlic bread and grilled tomatoes lingers like a good mood. Just like Su-ae said, the spaghetti is delicious. The noodles are cooked al dente, and the mussels and shrimp taste fresh. Su-ae dips her garlic bread in the red sauce.

"Good, isn't it?"

"It is."

"A lot of work today, right?"

"No, it was fine. But what about tomorrow? Are we going to the farm again?"

"Just me. We can't keep the flower shop closed two days in a row."

Papaya palms, a cat with a face twisted from a scar, Indonesian workers, the ficus trees. It's only been two hours since they came back from the farm but it all feels like a long time ago. After winding the last strands of spaghetti around the prongs of her fork, San puts her utensil down.

It happens when they leave Pomodoro and are walking from Gwanghwamun to Jongno.

From behind them, someone calls Su-ae's name. A tall man, about three or four years older. Su-ae looks up uninterested at first but soon her eyes gleam.

"Long time no see!"

Su-ae grabs the man's arm.

The man suggests they get a drink, and Su-ae turns to San. After all, they'd been thinking about where they could go next. Since she doesn't care where they go if they're not going back to the apartment, San nods, and Su-ae's face breaks into a smile.

Night descends. The trees along the avenues, exhausted from the day's sun, still look tired in the dark. A car passes by with its windows down, blasting loud music. Before anyone can turn and ask, What's up with that, the car accelerates and disappears around a corner. The light from buildings spills into the streets. The man says there's a café he likes, and he leads the way while the two women hasten to catch up with him. Pedestrians swerve to avoid them.

At the entrance hangs a photograph of the late conductor Karajan. The café is fittingly named La Muse. Karajan stands with his eyes closed and his lips firmly shut. The image is so vivid that it seems a whirlwind of sound might arise from his conductor's baton at any moment. In the middle of the establishment is a large table, with four more tables next to the walls. A small café structured so that anyone can see the dishes being washed in the kitchen. As they walk past Karajan and try to decide where to sit, the door opens again and San happens to make eye contact with the man who enters. The man exclaims, "Hey," and San averts her gaze, thinking she ought to know who this man is. She looks up again; he's smiling as if he's glad to see her, but she does not recognize him. He's not alone. There are two more men with him. Even when he pushes his companions aside to come up to her and says, "It's me," she can't quite recall who he is.

"You know, violets."

Violets? The photographer?

Only then does she go, Oh, right . . . But she still doesn't take his proffered hand.

Withdrawing his handshake, the man introduces his companions. San, having no choice, introduces her table as well. Su-ae says of the man they ran into on the street, "He's my friend." They decide to sit as one large party at the middle table.

"What do you mean by violets?"

"Violets? You mean swallow flowers?"

The photographer turns and says to one of his companions, "Hey, flower professor. Aren't you writing the cover story for this issue?"

The companion, sitting two seats away from him, nods. The photographer says, "This man knows everything there is to know about flowers. So tell us, what are you going to say about violets?"

"This and that, and how some call them the 'eyes of Io.'"

"Io? What?"

"She was a tragic woman in Greek mythology. Daughter of the river god Inachus. Zeus, the greatest god and a notorious womanizer, fell in love with her. Io went out for a walk one day and he covered the sky with clouds and had his way with her. But his wife Hera was a jealous god, and she got suspicious when clouds suddenly gathered at a certain spot, so she went to investigate. Zeus quickly rolled back the clouds and turned Io into a cow to fool Hera. The saddest part of this story is when Io, now a white cow, meets her father. The river god doesn't recognize her. How could he? She's been turned into a cow. He thinks she's cute and pats her back, not knowing this is the daughter he's searching for. And the more Io tries to tell him she's his daughter, the more she moos. Io manages to tell her father who she is by scratching out letters in the dirt with her hoof."

"A sad story. But what does this Io woman have to do with violets?"

"Zeus must've felt sorry to see the woman he loved as a cow eating grass, so he made flowers bloom around her in the image of her eyes. Those are white violets. Io's eyes. The poor girl went through so much strife. The Ionian Sea is named after her. She had to cross it as a cow. Only when Zeus and Hera reconciled was she returned to her human form."

The man described as a professor of flowers goes on to talk about the different stories from the East and West having to do with violets.

"Purple violets are the color of congealed blood. Believers make garlands of violets to lay on the altar of the Virgin Mary. Because when Christ was crucified, a violet shadow fell over the cross. The purple robes of Christian funerals, the amethysts worn by widows — that's all from violets. The flowers are very finicky. They wilt in too much sun, and when you water them, you have to avoid getting water on their leaves or petals. And a fun fact is that their leaves make roots. If you take a leaf and put it in water, it grows roots."

Su-ae stares at the professor. Someone stops him and asks the photographer, "What were you saying about the violets earlier?"

"Oh, I took some photographs of violets at a flower shop. She's the one who helped me."

"Ah — I thought you'd done something fucked up as usual."

Loud, lively talk. San finds herself buried in the conversation. Even now, the man is simply someone who came to photograph violets that one time. Right now, San doesn't care that she's a mess from having worked on the farm all day and that her clothes are dusty and dirty. Or that they smell. The summer night is humid and her body is tired. All she wants is to go back to her apartment, shower, and sleep. But in less than ten minutes, the man is going to shatter her indifference.

It happens when the tea is replaced by beer. Or to be more precise, when the table lift their glasses and toast, To new friends! Suddenly, the man puts his glass down and turns to San.

"Look, I have something to say. I'm not the kind of guy who says things like this but if I'm being honest, do you have any idea how fast my heart was beating when I saw you the first time with those damn violets? When I was looking at you through the viewfinder and you were looking down, I kept thinking about how beautiful your eyelashes were, the most beautiful in the world. I bet you didn't know that's what I was thinking?"

His confession makes the whole world seem like it's gone underwater. Even Su-ae, who'd been conversing with the friend they'd bumped into in the street, takes a closer look at San's eyelashes. No one at the table is more surprised than San. Every sound in the room dies down and soon falls completely silent. The clashing of beer mugs, the sound of people entering the café, the voices of the other patrons, the music — it all stops. Like the world has been paused. It would've helped if someone had said something to break the spell, but no one speaks. Finally someone points to her rising blush and teases her, saying, "Look at that, her face is turning red."

San tries to laugh, but awkwardness overwhelms her. The photographer's face, where she could look emotionlessly until mere seconds ago, suddenly becomes too much for her to bear. The only thing she manages through her embarrassment is, "Well, men just say whatever they want; what stopped you then?" She barely understands what she means herself.

One of the men asks, "So you're saying women can't?"

She replies, "Well, women, the thing about women is . . ." But her face is completely red and she bows her head.

The conversation moves on but her heart feels like it's swollen to twice its size. On occasion the man brushes back a lock of hair that keeps falling on his forehead, but he never looks in her direction or says anything else. Perhaps he's exhausted from going around taking photographs in the heat all day. He simply sits and drinks his beer. Only after some minutes does San risk looking at him. Jeans torn here and there, a dark persimmon-colored V-neck shirt. A muscular neck rising above the V. His hair is a little long, flowing freely down below his ears, and his arms are tan and firm where they emerge from his short sleeves. When he gets up to go to the bathroom, one of his companions, who is bald, leans over close enough for his whisper to tickle her face.

"Don't pay any attention to him, miss. That bastard is already stringing along three lovers, each as pretty as you are. He's like that to everyone. A lady-killer."

When the man returns to his seat, he's as expressionless as ever. Acting as if he'd never even spoken. What he blurted out merely ten minutes ago, *When I saw you the first time with those damn violets* . . . No one seems to be giving it a second thought. The group sits together but they're all having separate conversations. Just refilling their beer mugs from time to time. San clutches her mug and listens to them talk. There must be an imminent deadline at the magazine as the conversation is mostly about getting a photo of something for such and such column, advice for going on a field trip with naturalists to get wildflower shots, something about a spread that needs to be finalized by tomorrow. Su-ae is gossiping about people San doesn't know with the man they met on the street. When one person's conversation ends, another's begins. Su-ae sips her beer and occasionally glances at San, worried, as if asking, Why are you still sitting like that?

San, stuck between the photographer's friend and the man Su-ae met on the street, is unable to join any of the conversations. The man who'd said, *Don't pay any attention to him* . . . *he's a lady-killer*, sneaks a look at her. San is unaware she's being watched. Tamping down the maelstrom of emotions is taking all her concentration. What a strange day it's been. On the farm, she was overwhelmed by the rippling green of the ficus. The two orphaned papaya trees, the scar-faced cat that understands what people say as it drags its pregnant belly on the ground, Huyaya and Nadang —these images fill her mind's eye. Su-ae's unexpected confession regarding the farm owner. Sitting there alone between the others, she feels like a panting flower that's been trapped in the heat all day.

How much time has passed?

The man they met on the street tells Su-ae he has to go, and he gets up. Apparently he has an appointment with someone in Jongno. It's someone Su-ae is also acquainted with, and he asks her if she'd like to come with him. They'd be happy to see her. Su-ae looks at San again. San tells her to go ahead. "I'm just going home," she adds. The fatigue is about to overwhelm her, and all she wants to do is to go back to the apartment and wash her hair and body and cut her nails. When they rise, the men rise with them. Only the photographer doesn't get up as he stares at San's half-empty mug. Then he gulps down her remaining beer in one swig and goes to the counter to pay. Su-ae tries to divide the bill, but the photographer insists on paying for the whole thing.

"So sorry to put you out on our first meeting," says Su-ae, and the man waves away her words.

The night is balmy. Women in shorts fan themselves with their hands as they pass by along the tree-lined avenues.

They're saying their goodbyes in front of the café.

The photographer stretches out his hand and lays it on San's shoulder. Chills, despite the summer heat, run down her arm.

"You must be cold."

He sweeps over the goosebumps on her arm.

In that brief moment, she almost bursts into tears. She doesn't understand, right away, what this feeling means. On that hot, loud summer night awash in neon lights, Su-ae glances knowingly at the man sweeping his hand down San's arm. She caught the faint smile of the man who had leaned toward San and warned her about the photographer. They part ways. The photographer and his colleagues head toward the Salvation Army building, Su-ae and her male friend toward Jongno, and San in the direction of the Sejong Arts Center fountain.

The fountain is surrounded by crowds. There are no empty benches. College students nurse cans of beer as they sit on the ground, and laughter issues from a group of young women sitting off at a distance. A man sits in front of the fountain with his arms crossed. As she walks through the crowd, staring at the arching jets of water, someone grabs her arm. Who has returned for her? It's him.

"You looked like you were alone so I came back."

Even at this point it doesn't seem like she feels anything for him. Trying to keep her eyes open, she looks as if she can't understand how his reasoning makes any kind of sense.

"Would you have another beer with me?"

She shakes her head. "No."

Then, sorry to have refused so bluntly, she adds, "I'm just so tired. I had a lot of work to do today."

"Then sit with me for a while over there."

He's pointing to a wooden bench by the fountain. A couple, sticking together despite the heat, are getting up. The man strides over and sits down. San just stands there, so he gestures for her to join him. When she hesitates, he says, "Really, come on over here." San goes and sits down next to him.

"Why didn't you come for your photo?"

Photo?

"I've developed it and put it in my bag; come get it anytime."

He doesn't say anything more. Or move, at all. There's just a deep sigh from time to time. The man doesn't look as if he's staring at anything in particular; his gaze is empty.

How much time has passed?

"I have to go," says San as she rises, and he grabs her hand.

"May I love you?"

The sudden question drowns out the swish of the fountain's water, only to be replaced by the claxon of traffic. Not everyone can say such things so baldly. Such words can only be said by someone who has never known pain. The words make not San but the people sitting on nearby benches react with surprise. They watch, waiting for her to reply.

The man lets go of her hand and stands up.

"Let's go to the ocean sometime."

He bends over and kisses her on the cheek, and walks away past the fountain. It all happens in a moment. San stands where she is for a while. Is it her fatigue? She doesn't notice the people on the next bench watching her. Her palm wipes the spot on her cheek where he kissed her, and she bows her head as she trudges away. After walking through the underground passageway, she is suddenly too tired to take even one more step, so she takes the 104 bus. The bus is empty but she doesn't sit down. Perhaps she's afraid she's so tired she would never stand up again. In any case, at this point, she doesn't seem aware of what is happening in her heart.

She gets off at the bus stop beneath the ginkgo trees and crosses the street. She is so tired that even when she sees her landlady open her door and run out into the road, San is incapable of giving it a second thought. In the shadows, the landlady covers her face with her hands. Behind her comes her daughter shouting, "Mom!" San has one foot on the stairs going up to the long room when the landlord comes running out, chasing the landlady and her daughter. The man is barefoot and livid, kicking the folding tables in front of him as he runs. The pile of tables collapses and the children inside the annex cry at the top of their lungs. She hears their cries as she showers. She washes her hair, suds up the washcloth, and scrubs her back and calves. She's put on lotion and is cutting her nails when, struck with a thought, she kneels down and puts her ear on the floor. She's listening carefully. On the way home from school, she remembers, a little girl she knew would make San listen carefully like this, her ear on a grave. What a strange day. The girl she had remembered at the dike on the farm has followed her all day. A girl whom she can barely remember now. Curling up with her ear still to the floor, she falls into a deep sleep even before her hair can dry.

The Man Inside Her

She tries leaning a bit in her chair.

At first, she was sitting there alone looking out the window. But with the pattering rain, she soon felt the man's presence. No. It happened much earlier. The evening before, after falling asleep instantly, she had woken up just past midnight and had since then remained in a strange half-slumbering state. When her mind was a bit clearer, she listened for footsteps on the stairs. Yet Su-ae never came home. After a series of dizzying half dreams she was finally slipping into oblivion near dawn, but she was unable to keep herself under and washed up into consciousness once again. When she opened her eyes, she felt as if the man were gently bent over her.

"Are you getting up?"

He was smiling a little. As if he'd been waiting for her to wake. She closed her eyes to ignore this illusion, and that briefly made him disappear. But he hadn't disappeared; had he gone to the chair by the window? She finally fell asleep. But when she opened her eyes and felt she saw his face, she was so surprised she started upright in bed. Why did she keep thinking of him? Stumbling, she moved to the chair, feeling like she was sitting down not on the hard seat but on the man's knees.

It's raining.

The emptiness made her mumble out loud, but her cheeks moved more than her lips. Her sensitivity to rain or wind, or to any form of precipitation, annoyed her. Only in that moment of annoyance did she forget, for the first time since waking, about the man. And so even if he'd been sitting in that chair, he was briefly distanced from her. But then he approached again, little by little, and slipped into her body. There was no one there to see her but she felt the heat on her face as she blushed. Her embarrassment brought tears to her eyes. To cool herself, she rubbed her face with her palms but the heat only spread up to her forehead. So here she is now, trying to banish the man from her body, leaning away from him and the window.

But the man refuses to leave and simply leans in the same direction with her. As he leans, he makes an O with his thumb and middle finger and flicks her cheek like it's a guitar string, making her tumble out of the chair. She stares at the knocked-over chair like she's staring at the spectacle of herself on the floor, and goes to the pouch hanging on the fridge. The herbs growing on the windowsill watch as she rummages through it.

This man, who has deluged her consciousness like a swollen river in the night. San, who drowns because of him.

For a moment she stands still and looks toward Su-ae's bed past the sliding doors. Su-ae didn't return last night. She finally called San at dawn, saying she had been hanging out with her old friends all night, that she had kept thinking she was going to come back soon but then day broke, that she was calling from a hangover stew place. Su-ae said she would go directly to the flower shop after the hangover stew. That there was no way she could make it to the farm today.

San finds her membership card and locker key for the swimming pool, and runs outside into the rain without thinking of grabbing an umbrella. Drops of rain fall on her flushed forehead and eyebrows, stinging her skin. The fever is washed away by the cold droplets, but now the rain tickles so much she's about to cry.

How could that man have entered me like this?

She stretches out her hand to brush against the ginkgo trees as she runs.

That man she hadn't even recognized when they bumped into each other at La Muse—how can he have done this to her, overnight?

The droplets filtering through the green fans drench her hair and her face.

They soak into her skin, which makes her feel as if the man inside is getting drenched alongside her. Anxiety boils up. Her shoes slap forcefully against the wet pavement. The feeling swells like a cloud of tadpoles rising up from muddy water. When she's at the swimming pool, she slides open and walks through the door labeled "Women's Locker Room." Her white shirt and blue jeans are plastered to her skin. Hanging up her wet clothes, she rinses off her body in the showers and changes into her swimsuit. As soon as she enters the door to the pool, she lowers the goggles to cover her eyes. The swimming pool turns several shades darker.

Is it because of the rain?

Even accounting for the early hour, there would normally be a few other people diving into the water, but today there is only a man swimming alone in a far lane. She bends her knees and jumps up and down a few times to warm up. The man on the other side of the pool is swimming fiercely with a butterfly stroke; his gaze is like that of a skyborne hawk searching for a chicken, and his movements make the water around him arc and split into multiple angles. She waits until the man has swum to the other end of the pool before lowering herself in using the ladder. The blue-and-white tiled floor gives the water a deep cerulean hue. Briefly, she stands there with her body immersed in the cool water. Her flesh readily accepts the cold—nothing in this moment is more real than this coldness. Then, she puts her face into the water and slowly sinks to the floor. As if hiding from something.

She surfaces again.

Stretching out on top of the water, she kicks her legs as she strokes with her arms. Her body twists to face the ceiling, and the strokes of her arms adjust to the position. On the ceiling are vents and little windows, the size of bojagi wrapping cloths, through which she can see the sky outside. The panes are studded with droplets. The man who followed her as she ran through the rain to the pool and slid open the door that said "Women's Locker Room" did not, out of some sense of decorum, follow her inside. But there he is now, outside the windows up above, suspended in the rainy sky, staring down at her as she moves her arms in regular strokes. Her panic makes her breathe in instead of out, drawing water into her nose. She flips on her stomach, turns into a frog, and darts through the water to get away from him. The water inside her nose feels like a hammer hitting her face. In pain, she surfaces and clings to the edge of the pool like a tadpole, trying to catch her breath, when the man from the other lane emerges and swiftly walks past her toward the men's locker room. The farther he goes, the less she sees of his dripping form, his head disappearing first, followed by his torso, and then all she can see are his legs. A pale man. His thighs and calves are muscular but pale, with black hair. Hit with the premonition that the faceless man might suddenly whip around, she tears her gaze from his legs and lies down flat once more on the water.

Meeting him yesterday was a coincidence.

Once more, she moves her arms to propel herself through the water. There's a day she cannot remember, on which she met the man for the first time. A day that's disappeared from her memory. Only yesterday is alive to her now. Yesterday, I wore a plum-colored silk blouse and a light green skirt with a pattern of white droplets, she thinks, but then shakes her head in the water. No. I was wearing a plain white T-shirt and blue jeans. Enveloped in water, she becomes sad. Her thoughts are twisting the facts. I don't even own a plum-colored silk blouse or a light green skirt. In any case, she draws a line demarcating the time before she met the man again, and the time after. The split marks a completely new era. In the pool, she sweeps down her right arm with her left hand. Tiny seedlike goosebumps appear, just like when the man touched her arm yesterday.

How he caressed the countless goosebumps on her arm.

A photographer.

In the water, she tries to remember what it was like when they first met. Back when she wiped down the flower shop windows at every opportunity, or watered the plants on the pavement every half hour. Or was it one of those days when the monsoon rains would hastily pass over the city? When the farm owner telephoned her, speaking through the young man, he'd said she needed to help the photographer. She hadn't known what the man's work was exactly, so she waited for his instructions. The camera in his hands. The moment when he said, *Wait*, making her stand looking down as he repeatedly pressed the shutter down on her.

Panting—*hu hu*—she lies down again on the water.

At La Muse, when the tea had been replaced with beer, the unexpected words he had spouted: *I'm not the kind of guy who says things like this but if I'm being honest, do you have any idea how my heart was beating when I saw you the first time with those damn violets?* That moment when everything fell silent, when all sound disappeared from the world. Even the music from the café speakers seemed to break off before reaching her ears.

Using all her might, she sweeps the surface of the water with her arms. As if to sweep away all the thoughts that plague her mind.

Which ones are the violets? The man's indifferent voice. The man, upon having a pot of violets placed in front of him, had scowled. *So these are violets?* Almost yelling, incredulous, as if violets were some other thing and she had brought him the wrong plant.

But that man, who had once meandered past her life without making any impression, is now springing to life as she cuts through the water.

The man who put the pot on the flower shop table, then the pavement outside, constantly clicking his shutter. Complaining: *What's so pretty about these flowers? Such nonsense.* Their eyes had met and his voice had been accusatory: *Do you like these flowers too, miss?*

The man enraged at the mere thought of taking blame, muttering the whole time as he photographed from this angle, that angle. *Hey darling, if you want those photos of you, call me at this number.* The card he had given her.

Her face breaks the surface.

His card?

Somewhere in the flower shop is his card.

She almost leaps out of the water.

As she leaves to reenter the rain, the man whispers, Don't get wet. It's a cold rain, you'll catch your death. She stands underneath an awning. The throbbing instinct has cooled down now. The man doesn't try to touch her cheek or brush back the hair that falls across her forehead. He only gazes in the direction she gazes, worrying, warning that she should not get wet, since if she comes out of a hot shower and gets soaked in the cold rain, she'll catch a fever.

She runs to a newspaper stand.

She pants as she points to the plastic umbrellas, and the vendor stops arranging his newspapers and takes one of the many out, hands it to her, and takes her money. The rain patters down on the blue plastic of her unfurled umbrella. The woman who ran out into the street at dawn and the one who is now walking calmly through the rain, holding a plastic umbrella—are these the same woman? Their faces are too different.

She keeps mumbling as she walks. Last night. Last night, last night . . .

The goosebumps that rose when he put his hand on her. The feeling she would burst into tears when he swept his hand down her arm and said, *You must be cold*. Walking in the rain now, she thinks she knows what this feeling is. On other days she would've had to count one, two, three . . . to about forty before looking up at the ceiling, but today she opened her eyes as soon as she woke, and the hallucination of that man has been with her from that moment and is with her still. There was a face on the ceiling. The man's face. Did he watch me while I slept? She had drawn her blanket to her chin. Her sadness had swelled inside her. It had taken a long time for it to die down but, Ah, what's this. This vision of him that will not leave her side.

Just like when she left the apartment to go to the swimming pool, she breaks into a run, this time holding up the umbrella. The trees and buildings along the street whip past her. She runs past the people going to work. She runs as if trying to shake off the man.

The flower shop is already open.

New lilies crowd the blue buckets. Though Su-ae called from a hangover stew place, she must've dropped by the flower market on her way back. As soon as San arrives, out of breath, Su-ae looks up from her plant watering.

"I'm sorry I didn't come in last night!"

She seems awfully chipper for someone who hasn't slept a wink. San leaves Su-ae's words behind as she goes straight to the metal table, takes out the box of business cards, and rummages through it.

"What are you looking for?"

San doesn't look up.

"I said, what are you looking for?"

"A business card . . ."

"Whose?"

". . ."

"The guy from yesterday's?"

Su-ae chatters on about how the guy was no good, obviously some womanizer. She hoses San's calves as a prank. When San barely reacts, Su-ae hums as she finishes filling up the buckets with water and goes to shut off the tap. San shuffles through countless cards until she finds the man's and stares at his name. The man is the photographer at *Flower World*. She slips his card into her notepad.

All she does that morning is gaze at the lilies in the blue buckets, even when the rain has stopped. From time to time, Su-ae throws her a concerned glance. She comes up to her and asks, "Are you feeling all right?"

San shakes her head.

Hesitant, Su-ae asks, "What's wrong?"

San only looks at her mutely, and Su-ae tilts her head. San has stared at the lilies so hard that their whiteness pierces her eyes when she closes her lids. An endless space appears before her, like she's slipping into an abyss.

As San moves the weeping figs, sago palms, rubber plants, and orchids outside, she stumbles and scrapes her knee. It happens in a flash. Red droplets dot her knee like dew. Where has this sunlight been hiding? A shard of it falls across her scratched skin and quivers there in pieces.

Su-ae taps her shoulder. "Are you worried about something?"

After putting on some ointment and a Band-Aid, San stares at the lilies again. Su-ae sounds as if she's assuaging a child throwing a tantrum. San feels her brain sloshing from side to side as she shakes her head no.

"You're not telling me what's wrong. You're weird today. What are you thinking about? You look like some sick person. Like your body is here but not your thoughts. What's going on? Did something happen yesterday? Look at your face. You're completely pale! Come on, you've got to tell me what's up with you."

". . ."

"Look, just snap out of it!"

"I just have a headache."

"A headache?"

"Yes . . . It's bad. I can't think. It's like I'm floating in midair. I think I'll go for a walk."

"Do you think a walk will do it? Maybe take a pill. Or go see a doctor, no?"

"I think I'll be fine with some air."

San glances at the shadows falling across on Su-ae's neck as Su-ae replies, "You do that."

She steps out of the flower shop.

Ah.

The rain has passed, and the sunlight bouncing off the windows of the bakery across the street is so intense she can't help but let out a deep sigh.

"Mom, look! A rainbow!"

A girl with a short bob pulls her mother by the hand and points to the sky. A delivery boy emerges from the bakery, bag slung over one shoulder, and says, "Wow, a real rainbow." Their exclamations cause San to shield her eyes and look up as well. The sky practically pours its blue color onto her face. A real rainbow. Unbelieving, her eyes blink as they get teary. A dull ache blooms in her chest. It's the sorrow of being unable to follow, the regret of being unable to take off after. A far, far-off longing. Not knowing where she's going, San begins to walk.

In the place where a high school used to be, there's now an art museum—she stops in her tracks and looks into the grounds. At

129

the other end of some granite steps, there's a new building being constructed in an empty lot. An excavator stands guard there, looking like an open-mouthed beast. The wide mouth seems to draw her in as she dazedly enters the museum grounds, where she falls into a sitting position in the middle of the path. A puddle soaks her skirt. Uncaring, she remains seated.

A little way off, construction workers in red hard hats are leaning against a yellow fence and smoking, staring into another part of the museum grounds where two women are playing badminton. Have the women brought their badminton set from somewhere? Under their tight, above-the-knee denim skirts, their legs move busily. If it weren't for their constant movement, the entire scene, including the art museum, would look like a tableau.

Having inserted herself into the tableau, San manages to heave herself back up to a standing position and walks toward one of the trees to crouch under it. Such vivid white legs. Hugging her knees, she stares at the girls playing badminton, just like the construction workers. Not at the shuttlecock that flies through the air like a sparrow, nor their hair or faces or breasts, but at their dynamic legs, squinting at them from the shade.

"Don't cry."

Only when the man inside her whispers to her does she realize she's been crying while staring.

"Get away from me."

Her hand pushes at him through thin air. What's wrong with me? Her heart sinks. The man's voice saying, Don't cry, had been so clear that she turned around to look, but no one is there. Only trembling leaves, shaking off rain droplets.

The slender legs of the badminton girls move with such alacrity, like fish whipping through water, and the girls' shoes slide smoothly over the sand. When they pick up dropped shuttles, their skirts hike dangerously up their legs. Almost revealing their behinds. San feels such a surge of excitement that she hurriedly diverts her gaze to the construction workers.

"That bitch, that foxy bitch!"

"She knows we're watching; she's egging us on!"

"Ah, they're cute; leave them alone! Do you think any of us can get a show like that for free? I feel less tired already!"

"What a horny little devil you are."

"Even when I'm just looking?"

It's unbearable, so she gets up. One of the construction workers tosses his cigarette to the ground and looks in her direction. His glance is so unsettling she wraps her flower-print skirt around her legs and quickly makes her way down to the sidewalk.

He's a photographer.

She looks down like when she first met him and smiles shyly.

He's a photographer.

She looks up at the sky and turns her head slightly to the side.

He's a photographer.

She lets her butt stick out as she looks at a seafood restaurant's streetside aquarium, inspecting the fish inside.

He's a photographer.

She stops in front of a movie theater and looks at a poster of a pretty actress holding a gun.

Whenever she pauses, she feels as if the man is taking her photo, and so these interruptions in her walk are posed and unnatural.

San stands across from the address on the man's business card. The man who breathed with her, inside of her, the ghost of the real man inside that building, makes a run for it as soon as she stops in her tracks. Left alone, she stares for a long time at the building.

As she stands there, she realizes what it is she wants to do in that moment, but gives up. If I call him, he'll mock me. The thought makes her anxious, and her retreat into a café is a pathetic one. She looks as if she's about to collapse. She finds a table where she can't see the building, and falls into one of the seats. Coffee is brought to her and the music changes. For the first time since sitting down, she raises her gaze, focusing on a speaker in a corner of the café.

A crescent moon as slight as your eyelash falls into the forest
A dawn having spent all night at the bottom of a tall wall,
    crying
From the bottom of a tall wall, tall wall, tall wall, tall wall,
    tall wall, tall wall
A dawn that rises having cried all night

The tears appear so rapidly she has to press her eyes with her sleeve. Pushing away the teacup, she buries her head in her arms, in a patch of soft sunlight. She feels as if she is observing herself. The observing San knows well the San that has put her head down. She knows that the latter San, crying into the tabletop, has been possessed by something since last night. That in the course of this possession, she has become indifferent to almost everything else. She's being foolish. Bumping into everything in her path. Talking even more slowly than before, her eyes out of focus. Looking at something but not really seeing it. Mourning, but smiling when prompted. As if angry at this observing self, the corporeal self suddenly raises her head. The corporeal self is anxious, in a way the observing self has never seen before. It surprises her so much, she evaporates.

San walks back the way she came.

"Are you feeling any better?"

At the flower shop, Su-ae is careful with her friend, and San nods absentmindedly.

"Look, I think I have to get back to the farm. You stay here. We can't close the flower shop two days in a row, right?"

San is so caught up in her own thoughts that she doesn't answer. Su-ae says, "Well, you keep an eye on things over here. I'll go alone."

San doesn't answer. Even when Su-ae looks her directly in the eye and says, "Hey! Are you really, really okay?"

"Look at this."

Su-ae loudly makes a fuss, trying to get San's attention, and pulls at her arm. When San looks to where Su-ae is pointing, her eyes grow wide. There's a moth trapped between two green leaves. Not just wedged there but properly caught by the plant.

"It's a Venus's eyelash!"

"Venus's eyelash?"

"They're also known as Venus flytraps. A carnivorous plant."

"Carnivorous plant?"

"Exactly. A plant that eats insects, like a sundew. Weirdly I kept seeing mosquitoes buzzing around over there and wondered about it. It was these guys all along."

These guys? Su-ae's expression makes her smile.

"How does a plant eat an insect?"

"I guess it's a bit strange. But they do, and that's what makes them carnivorous. There are others that eat little mammals like rats. They have separate organs for digestion. Some have hairs growing toward an opening so that insects slip in and never make their way out again."

Carnivorous plants.

San peers through the eyelashes of the Venus flytrap. A moth, hopelessly struggling in its snare. She had no idea that there were plants that eat insects. And to think some even eat rats. When she touches it, the mouth-shaped trap flexes. She takes the plant to a spot in the sun and is still staring at it when Su-ae gets ready to leave.

"Why do you keep staring at it? Do you want one of your own? They're not easy to keep. Clouds of insects everywhere they grow. They give off a scent to draw the insects. A friend of mine grows them on her balcony and, wow, the mosquitoes and the bugs and the flies. It takes all kinds to make a world. When I asked what the hell she was doing with them, she said looking at them made her think she wanted to live. Something about the plants growing in wastelands but being so beautiful. Some people grow carnivorous plants and keep them as pets. They eat up mosquitoes and thrive on neglect. Those Venus's eyelashes will grow pretty big in a few days, you'll see."

Now alone in the flower shop, San walks by the sago palms and orchids looking for other pots of carnivorous plants. Plants that survive in wastelands. She goes back to the Venus's eyelash in the sunny spot and peers into it. Little by little, the plant is eating the moth caught in its jaws.

Nothing Happened This Past Summer

The afternoon crawls by.

San waters the plants out on the sidewalk, wipes down the windows, and, from time to time, takes out the business card in her pocket and stares at it. When she remembers, she also checks up on the carnivorous plant that's still ingesting its meal of moth.

The sun quickly sucks up the water on the windows and on the street. The sidewalk is parched, no matter how often she waters it. When she's making tea for herself, the man is there with her, and when she's having her lunch at the conveyor-belt sushi place, putting a piece of shrimp sushi into her mouth, he's right by her side. There she is, arranging chrysanthemums into a wreath instead of the roses that were ordered. The man comes up to her and whispers, That's not the right one, and picks up a rose for her. She drops the flower and sits there, still. From her pocket she takes out his business card again before going to the phone on top of the drafting table. She lifts the receiver and dials the man's number on the card. All she has to do is press this number and she'll hear his voice? Her excitement slowly turns to apprehension before she presses the last digit, and she puts down the receiver. Fear flickers on her pale face. Her eyes must feel strained because she begins pressing down on the area around them, moving on to massage her whole face. What the hell am I doing, she shouts at herself. He was nothing to me but now I've given him my heart. Was I always this fragile a woman? But she cannot escape her hallucination. She struggles for a while with her desire. Unexpectedly, she dials Choi's number instead, the one written on her notepad. Choi's familiar voice on the other end goes, Hello?

"Hello?"

After listening to him repeat the word a few times, she quietly replaces the phone. San stares at the photographer's phone number again as if to bore through the cardboard with her intensity. Now she doesn't even need the card; the number is engraved in her mind.

She goes outside and sprinkles the plants with water one more time. The sunlight, as if lying in wait, pounces and sucks the moisture away again. As she battles with her urge to call the man, she tears up once more. What is the point of calling him? What would they do if they sat across from each other? Her heart sinks.

What is this thing that's dragging her around? His confession? Or does she love him now? The two questions make her lean her forehead against a purple sago palm. The tedium of summer must have been digging a trap this whole time. Love, all of a sudden.

Evening descends again and she's closing the shop shutters on her own. Su-ae hasn't returned from the farm yet. She walks out into the street, the Venus flytrap in her hands.

San enters a stationery shop right before the Gwanghwamun intersection and buys a new notebook.

Carrying the plant and her notebook, she plods back to the apartment and puts down the carnivorous plant next to the herbs. Washing her face, she opens the windows of the long room and looks down at the ginkgo trees. It feels as if someone has sidled up right next to her, looking down with her, and she winces with an accompanying gesture as if to say, Back off. From some corner she brings out her ink bottle and fountain pen. *Violets*. Remembering something, she finds an English to Korean dictionary and comes back. Turning the onionskin pages, her gaze wanders around the definition of violets.

Violator: Noun, one who breaks rules, invades, insults, rapes
Violence: Noun, a disturbance, disruption, destruction
Violet: Noun, a plant, a swallow flower . . . purple, the color,
    also used to describe . . . an oversensitive person, a shy
    person ("shrinking violet")
Violin: Noun, a musical instrument . . . a player of, a violinist

As she reads on, her expression grows more and more disconcerted. San pushes away the dictionary and sits up neatly in front of her new notebook. After a long while, she leans forward and writes.

Nothing happened this past summer.

After this one sentence, she regards the expanse of the page for a while before adding one sentence after another.

Nothing happened this past summer. Only that, in the hot sun from time to time, a brief thought would appear and disappear around me. That thought was closer to me than any of the flowers in the shop. Even as I tried to capture the thought on paper, the heat would exhaust me and I'd give up. There were plenty of things I gave up on, using the heat as an excuse. Which means I spent this past summer repeatedly deciding to do things and then giving up on them. As if my life were an exhibition of how good I am at giving up. It was that kind of summer.

She stops writing and looks down at her notebook.
She wears an expression of amazement. She's amazed that she wrote something. To write about what went on this summer — she's burning with determination inside, making the idea seem

feasible. It seems feasible because she's decided, Let whatever happens happen. She's usually someone who makes little effort to assert her opinion, and the world often perplexes her. But there's always been the thought: If only I could write something . . . In the past, there was nothing she desired more. Yet this past summer, the desire to write has felt as if it belongs to someone else. When absolutely nothing stretched out in all directions, what could she even bother unveiling with the fine point of her pen that possibly meant anything? Writing had suddenly felt like an annoyance. So she hadn't written anything this summer.

Her dark eyes briefly pool before drying again. It's him. Her desire to write overflows, but she makes no progress. Several times she tries to recapture her thoughts but all she does is fruitlessly put nib to paper. Sweat beads on her forehead. In the end, she doesn't write a sentence more and places the pen down on the folded gutter. San hears steps coming up the narrow staircase. Is it Su-ae? But it's the recreation office door that's being unlocked. She grabs the pen and forces herself to bend over the notebook once more. Her forehead nearly touches the paper. Tears well and then disappear. To think that she was trying to hide herself from the hallucination shadowing her by writing.

It is now past midnight and nearing dawn.

San is sleeping with her face pressed into the notebook when she wakes to frantic knocking.

"Miss . . . miss!"

The landlady.

It's very loud outside. Are they fighting again? But it's not that. It's the sound of murmuring people, children crying, something being thrown about, wood splintering.

"Miss! Miss!"

The landlady is kicking at the door.

San becomes fully awake when she hears shouts of, Fire, Fire!

The landlady is desperately banging on the kitchen door now. When San opens it, the landlady gestures for her to leave.

"There's a fire. You must come with me."

"A fire?"

"Look . . . Come on!" The landlady grabs her hand. "Where is Miss Su-ae?"

"I think she's spending the night at the farm."

"Come on, then, let's go."

As soon as the landlady leads her out the kitchen door, the wail of sirens fills the air. In a bewildered panic, San shouts again, "What's happening?"

"There's a fire!"

San nearly trips on the stairs down. The landlady is a few steps ahead of her. Her eldest daughter hugs her piano, as if determined to block the flames with her own body. The youngest runs over to the landlady and tugs at her skirt. Hauling the folding tables in the corridor into the living room, the landlord takes one look at his wife and three daughters and shouts, "What are you standing there for? The tables will burn!"

Quickly, the landlady approaches the stacked tables. Her skirt is ripped from the youngest's grasp. The little one bursts into sobs.

"Be quiet! I can't think straight right now; stop that crying!"

The landlord's castigation only serves to amplify the child's cries.

"Don't cry, don't cry," says the middle daughter as she ushers the youngest away through the stacks. Where is this fire? San follows the two girls out into the street. She's hit by the smell of smoke. Despite the early hour, a concerned and murmuring crowd stands outside. San turns to see where the firefighters are aiming their hoses. It's the room across from her own, the recreation office.

It takes twenty minutes to tamp down the flames.

The street-facing windows reading "Recreation Office" are shattered and spewing smoke. Thankfully, the flames haven't spread anywhere else. The firefighters bring someone out on a stretcher, and the crowd moves in to see. San follows suit. It's the young man. The one who carries the guitar on his shoulder. Who played so maniacally in the Daehak-ro café. Whose performance under the flashing lights was as wild as those of the dancers.

Even with the fire out and the ambulance gone, the crowd mills about on the street, talking amongst themselves. San stands with them and looks up at the burned-out windows before going back inside. The landlord's family stand in the even more crowded courtyard and stare when she enters.

"What happened?"

At San's question, the landlady gives her a look suggesting, How on earth would I know?

"Well," the landlady says out loud, "at least that's the extent of the damage. Think of what might've happened if the fire had spread! Dear god, my heart is still thumping."

"Shouldn't we contact his family?"

"I don't know his family, but I did see a phone number he'd written down so I called that instead."

"Will he be all right?"

"Apparently he had a mind to die, setting that fire."

"What?"

"I don't know the details—they'll investigate it in the morning. Go inside and get some sleep. Oh, and I think you'll have to use the kitchen-side exit for the time being. They told me we can't go near the other side until they're done with their investigation."

When the landlord tells his daughters to go back to sleep, the little girls file into their shared bedroom. San watches the man take out a cigarette and light it before she goes up the narrow staircase and enters the long room through the kitchen door.

The open window lets in a breeze still tainted with smoke. For a moment, San looks down at the street. The murmuring crowd has dispersed. The lights are out in the café across the way. Only the ginkgos stand amongst the streetlamps. What did that mean? He had a mind to die? That singing young man, he was trying to kill himself? San closes the window.

She opens her front door. The fire must've stopped inside the recreation office as nothing seems amiss from the side of the landing. A white no-entry sign is hung on the door. No entry. She stares at the red letters for a moment. She can still see the flickering flames. It seems improbable the door is still standing. Her shoulders tremble. If the fire had burned the door and crossed the landing, it would've been a matter of seconds before it invaded the long room. Feeling tense, she puts on her shoes and goes to the other door. She pushes aside the sign and tries the doorknob. Without any resistance, the door opens.

She takes a step inside.

Shoes lie scattered in the foyer. The shoe stand must've been knocked over when the young man was being hauled out, but the fire did not otherwise reach the foyer. She takes another step inside. The smell of smoke assaults her eyes and mouth.

Even compared to the room she shares with Su-ae, this apartment is long. Shelves line the walls. Some shelves are incinerated and gone; others are still standing. Light shines through the shattered windows. Objects from the shelves are destroyed and scattered about on the ground. Only the foyer was saved; the fire has eaten nearly everything else. Burned speakers, burned CDs, burned guitars. The blackened table is flipped over, with pots and tables strewn about. The guitar the man previously carried on his shoulder is half-gone, the remaining half lying in pieces on the ground. A folding bed stands against one of the long walls, its sheets black.

San pauses for a moment and listens, spooked. A tiny whine has startled her. It's coming from under the bed. She looks down.

While the streetlamps are faintly visible through what remains of the windows, it's still very dark.

"It's you."

The dog that never left the man's side.

The dog that, when the man sang at Three Years Later, would stay caged outside by the chain-link fence.

She bends down and tries to pull out the whining dog. It's in so much shock that it refuses to leave.

"It's all right. Come on."

With her head almost completely under the bed, she manages to gather the dog in her arms. Its trembling is so violent she can feel it into her chest. "It's all right," she says as she gently strokes the dog. Still embracing it, she crouches down. The dog's ear, stomach, and tail are singed. She looks into its eyes and sees tears. Its eyes are full of terror. It's all right. She hugs the dog close to herself.

The dog suddenly kicks away. Running quickly over the shattered guitar and the blackened table legs, before San can even shout, No, the dog leaps out the window and down into the street. When she gets to the window, she sees it getting up from the asphalt and dash into the night. By the time she's past the scattered shoes and the white sign and down the narrow staircase, the dog has long disappeared.

If You Listen Carefully

As autumn arrives, San begins to behave even more like a fool. She stumbles on stairways and swims into the walls at the pool. Her already slow speech slows even more, and she answers the simplest questions with vague mumbles. She seems to be looking at something but isn't really looking at anything. On those occasions, her dark eyes seem sad but also absent.

When she opens the apartment door in the morning, she glances at the recreation office out of habit. On a brief impulse, she wants to enter the office. The nail heads and the words DO NOT ENTER make her want to break open the door. Even though all that's inside has been swept through by fire. Clearing her throat to calm her nerves, she turns away.

Outside the building, she looks up once more at the burned-out windows.

The apartment has been left the way it is, with only the sign forbidding people from entering. The singing man taken away in the ambulance never came back. According to the landlady, he is the son of an extremely wealthy household. She emphasized the word "extremely" when she said this. The son of the extremely wealthy household, who had also studied in New York, had quit his studies and taken up music despite his father's adamant opposition. As an act of rebellion against this father, who had subsequently cut him off, he had shorted the electricity and started a fire. In fact, the landlady had never rented out the room to the young man; he had just shown up one day and started living there. Later she learned that the official renters were acquaintances of the young man, and they had allowed him to stay in their office after he was cut off by his father, but now the renters denied any liability regarding the fire, and the landlady didn't know what to do.

San wanted to know just one thing: What happened to the man after he'd been taken away in an ambulance? The landlady had no news about him and kept talking about other things. That such and such came to investigate the fire, and such and such came to question her. That the singing man's father was a really famous person, and the landlady told San his name. San didn't know who he was. Just someone living in another world, as far as she was concerned. When the landlady said, Can you believe it, his father is taking care of two whole other children by another woman, San could only reply, Oh.

San wondered how the young man was doing, not about the details of his family life, but she didn't ask. All she had asked was why the recreation office still had their letters up on the window.

"Oh, that was put up by the previous-previous renter," said the landlady. A married couple whose job was to put on events for kindergartens or companies out on picnics. She had neglected to take down the letters when they moved out. San never heard about what happened to the singing man. The landlady seemed to have only heard whatever pieces of information the investigators had shared and didn't have any other news. The landlord eventually received generous compensation from the extremely wealthy father and nailed the office door shut and wrote DO NOT ENTER on it, never mentioning the matter again.

And then, except for the long room, the building was empty.

Around the time that gossip about the fire died down, the piano in the inner compound's living room appeared tossed out in the street, its lid smashed. The piano bench was flipped over with its four legs in the air. Su-ae opened the kitchen door and shouted, "Please keep it down!" But the landlord ignored her and repeatedly broke the bench. The eldest daughter, who had always hovered protectively around her piano, bit her father's thigh hard. As he raised his hand to strike his daughter, the landlady drove a wash-basin into his back with all her might. Only when the police arrived was the landlord's violence contained.

Late at night that same day the door resounded with loud knocks. As soon as Su-ae opened it, the landlady pushed into the room, begging them to let her hide. Her frantic eyes were blood-shot. There was a large scratch across her cheek right to her upper lip.

"Please, don't let me out of here," she said as she lowered her voice. "Because if you do, I might kill my husband. I'm scared of myself."

For four days, the landlady did nothing but sleep in the long room. The fact that the police had been summoned not by Su-ae or herself but by her daughter—this had put her into a state of shock. More than her husband destroying the piano, what really tortured her was the fact that her own daughter had called the police on her father. The landlady had lived thinking, I want my children to turn out right so I'm going to hold off on divorce, I'll leave when the kids grow up—but now she kept thinking, I've wounded my daughter in a way she'll never recover from, and this made her cry constant, silent tears. Every morning Su-ae or San would prepare a meal for her before they left, but when they came back home in the evenings, the food would be untouched. Su-ae would force her to have a mouthful of yogurt or a sip of mugwort tea. As the young women treated the scratch with ointment, the landlady gave herself over to their care begrudgingly. The task of telling the children fell to San. The middle and youngest children would come up to sit with their mother briefly but the eldest never visited. After about a week in the long room, where her days and nights melded into one, the landlady pulled herself together and took her daughters down to Daegu. Her note, saying she was going to her mother's house, was addressed not to her husband but to Su-ae.

It was September and the landlady had still not returned. The landlord had disappeared somewhere too. The building, save for the young women's long room, was either burned out or empty.

Down the street was another avenue lined with yellow ginkgo trees. Unlike on other streets, where there was enough sun to turn the leaves yellow, the dimness of their block kept their ginkgo trees green for longer. But their trees had no leaves at all now. When the fan-shaped leaves finally started to turn, Su-ae opened the window as soon as she woke up each morning. Even though it was still the time of year when bugs would stick to the screen at night, she would open the window, look down at the two lines of ginkgo trees along the street, and sigh deeply.

One day at dawn, Su-ae opens the window only halfway before shouting, "Oh my god!" A new smell hits San's face. San turns her head to the green smell of leaves. The ground is littered not just with yellow leaves but ones that are still green as well. The street cleaners are hitting the trees with long sticks to make all the leaves fall. The sound makes San and Su-ae look farther up ahead, where two street cleaners are sweeping up the leaves into still-green mounds. Getting over her surprise, Su-ae turns to the herbs and Venus flytrap and bids them good morning with a look. Saying, Well, I guess they do that because it would be a pain to sweep day after day. Their flourishing herbs fill the windowsill of the room. Late at night, Su-ae boils water and steeps tea with some of the herbs. San drinks some of her extra tea in the mornings. It is bitter on the tongue, but her head feels clearer after a cup.

"See you at the flower shop," says Su-ae to San as she packs her swim bag and heads down the stairs, waving at her from the street among the banks of fan-shaped leaves before disappearing. San has stopped going swimming.

As San walks to work, she looks up from time to time at the ginkgo trees. It's only on their street that the leaves were struck off; the ones elsewhere are still safe. All the way to Gwanghwamun, the yellow leaves tremble on the branches overhead.

Crossing through the underground passage, San makes her way toward Sejong Arts Center. The unopened storefronts glide by San like a stage set, until she stands in front of the flower shop. With a long sigh, she raises the shutters and steps inside. She puts a small pot of violets into a watering can, and she walks out into the street. Past the Saemoonan Church and Salvation Army building, through the lingering smell of coffee from Bonjour Restaurant. Past where there used to be a high school and is now an art museum. It's still early in the morning when she stands across from where the man works—the empty lot connected to the museum. It's a construction site, with earth piled up here and there. During the night someone must've kicked over the barricade announcing UNDER CONSTRUCTION. Ready to dig up, turn over, or consume anything in its path, the excavator—with its wide-open mouth—stands stoically in front of the fallen barricade. Aside from a few trees in the corner, it's a desolate site. The mounds of earth are made of sand, rocks hauled from a quarry, and disturbed soil. This is why the patch of white and purple, yellow and pink violets, twenty or so, immediately stands out. The morning breeze makes the whites and yellows and purples flutter in the same direction. At first glance they look like a city's public beautification efforts. San takes out her pot of violets from the watering can and plants them among the others. She presses down on the earth and fills up the can using a tap nearby. Carefully shielding the fluttering petals and leaves with her free hand, she waters them so only the roots get wet, each gesture imbued with intention and hope. Still holding the sprinkler, she stands and looks up at the building where the man works.

That man from the summertime, whom she'd unexpectedly met again one night. Ever since his confession—*do you have any idea how my heart was beating when I saw you the first time with those damn violets*—she hasn't had a moment's freedom.

Since the day she woke up and saw him, she's spent every moment with him. Today, just like yesterday, he drank tea with her in the morning and will be by her side during lunch. Not for a moment can she elude his presence.

She's kept his business card with her at all times. As summer wound down and fall began and he took up more and more of her inside, her heart started sinking at random times. Whenever she felt it slipping down, she would come to the lot and look up at the windows of his office. When summer ended, she began planting violets there.

After planting her newest round, she leaves the lot and mixes in with the people arriving at work. She stands at the crosswalk. She's come this way countless times but has never seen the man. Once, she even walked into his office building, right up to the door reading *Flower World*, but she did not bump into him.

Buoyed along by the tide of pedestrians, she crosses the street. Here too the ginkgo leaves are trembling in the morning breeze. She looks down and then up again at the buses running through the carpet of yellow. As the bus stops and men in neckties crowd off, she stares—and then turns away. It's as if a thought has suddenly occurred: What if he is among them?

She hurries as if she's been thrown out or is being chased. People have to avoid bumping into her. She's so intent on avoiding this potentially difficult moment—potentially running into the man—that her steps are clumsy in their haste, seconds away from smashing her nose or crashing her shoulder against someone. What's wrong with that woman? Some people turn and stare until she disappears from view.

Once she's put enough distance between herself and the building, her strength wanes and she slows down. She skirted his building hoping to bump into him, but now she's running away in case she does. As she plods toward the flower shop, pedestrians now avoid her for different reasons; she looks so fragile that a mere brush might send her toppling down.

At lunch, she once again stares up at the man's office before coming back to the flower shop. She doesn't reply to Su-ae, who asks where she's been. Neither does she respond to the question about whether she's had lunch at all, so that Su-ae looks San in the eye, flower shadows falling across her face.

Is it around 4:00 p.m.?

San takes out her notebook and is about to walk out of the shop when Su-ae grabs her.

"Where are you going?"

"Just for a walk. I'll be back soon."

"What's up with you these days?"

". . ."

"If you keep getting headaches, you should go see a doctor, not go on all these walks. You'll never get better!"

"A bit of a cool breeze makes me feel better."

San's eyes, not looking at anything in particular, suddenly quiver with tears; Su-ae lets go of her arm. If she were to insist that San stay, she would probably succeed. But how would that help San? As San walks away, Su-ae watches San's dragging gait with a concerned expression. San seems possessed. But also too innocent for Su-ae to get angry. Whenever she tries to make a point with San, her friend only replies, Really? And does not argue. Su-ae watches San swaying slightly as she walks off somewhere, then she leaves the flower shop unattended and sets out to follow her.

When San stops in front of the city art museum, Su-ae, at a distance, stops as well. San looks as if she's about to walk into the museum, but she sits down in a wooden chair in a nearby empty lot instead. The wind ruffles her skirt. Su-ae feels disconcerted as she watches San sit and do nothing.

Is San really out here for the breeze?

Su-ae begins to feel bad for trailing her friend. There's a ginkgo tree shading the wooden chair where San continues to sit. Su-ae is about to turn back when San gets up and walks toward Gyeonghuigung Palace. After a moment of hesitation, Su-ae follows. San goes around the palace's front gate and stops right at the crosswalk where the street leads up a hill toward the hospital. Even when the light changes, she stands there, staring up at a building across the street.

What exactly is she looking at?

Su-ae follows the direction of San's gaze. It's just an office building among other office buildings. Their mirrored surfaces reflect the same sky: a patch of clear blue with a dot of cloud. Curious as to what San is so intently focused on, Su-ae examines the building more closely. There's a fluttering banner with red letters out front, but there isn't anything visibly special.

San looks briefly as if she might stand there forever, but then she crosses the street.

Su-ae hurries after her. San glances back, making Su-ae jump out of her skin, but she doesn't seem to spot her in the crowd. On the ground floor is a café with large windows. San hesitates before going in. Su-ae watches her from outside, wondering if she's there to meet someone. There aren't many people inside, and most tables are empty. San takes a window seat. Behind her hangs a painting of two women wearing loose, white sleeveless shirts, running along a beach by the deep blue sea. Their hands almost touch, and their strong arms and firm calves could take them to the ends of the earth. Their hair flies freely in the wind behind San, who just sits there. People walk in from time to time, but no one takes the seat across from her.

Su-ae begins to worry about the shop she's left empty. To think she's followed San out the door, all the way here. San looks exhausted when a server comes to take her order. She must've ordered coffee as they presently put a mug down and leave her alone. San seems to have no intention of drinking it; she simply sits there and stares out into the street in the opposite direction from Su-ae. A little while later, she takes out the notebook wedged under her arm and lays it flat on the table. She moves as if to take a sip of coffee but grows still again. Giving up, Su-ae retraces her steps and returns to the flower shop.

Now no one watches over San.

Ever since her unrelenting desire for the man began, the observing San that had considered every move of the corporeal San has disappeared. The San who was sorrowful and yet would occasionally burst into laughter is also no more. And her will to communicate with the man by any means necessary has dissipated.

What remains is a woman in pitiful thrall, a small woman curled up at the bottom of a well, sitting in the café on the ground floor of the building where he works, ignored by all. Her minutely raised head reveals agitated, uncertain eyes. This movement is the only indication there is something of her still left inside.

San sits, trying to write something in the notebook. But she only holds her pen, gaze fixed somewhere beyond the window.

In time, she bends over the notebook and, as if using all her might, begins to write.

Last summer . . .

She turns to a fresh page and moves, again, her fingers gripping the pen.

In the heat of last summer, I could see with relative clarity the minari field. Perhaps the minari wasn't planted there; maybe it was a place where the minari always grew wild. The two girls there are nine or ten, maybe even eight, and since one of them is a younger me, it means this was all a long time ago. And considering what people preferred to cultivate back then, I think the minari field was a wild one. But for an untamed field it was just too wide. Green grassy plains stretching far away, in my memory. Maybe, yes, maybe the field was only a few pyeong, but my mind stretches it out to the horizon. I thought of that field obsessively. The minari was waist-high in water. March, April, or May. There was soft sunlight there. What were the two girls doing as they stared out into the scene? What were they doing when they began to take off their clothes? Since there was an irrigation ditch along the dike, perhaps they were playing around and fell into the water. I don't know why they took off their clothes, but I can clearly see the green spot on the back of that girl. It happened when they were lying on the grass growing on each side of the dike, which is why I thought it was a grass stain. Surrounded by green stalks, the small whiteness of her body. In my memory, only her body remains. Maybe in her memory, as well, she only holds mine. But in the heat of last summer, taking a snapshot of the minari, the body that I saw and the body she saw take form. She's the beautiful one. Because I loved that child. And wherever she ended up later, in that moment at least, she loved me. If this is the case, then if she were to remember where the minari grows, in her mind's eye I would be the beautiful one. That's what love is. At first, the girls lay on their stomachs and stared out at the green minari, propping up their heads on their elbows, swaying their feet in the air. If their ankle-bones hadn't crashed into each other, I never would've seen her young soft body. Still lying there, she stretched out her arm, pulled her foot in, and rubbed her anklebone, and I was fascinated by how her body curved to bring the foot into her grasp. It made me stop rubbing my own foot to stare. On her white back, the deep green spot curved as well. My palm stretched out to the spot but didn't cover it. My palm was small and her spot was wide. Last summer, what kept me together was this scene I never told anyone about, think-ing about it in the silence of the heat, making a certain joy wash over me. But what made me try to depict this scene in writing is not that soft joy. In the scene, my palm that hovered over her green spot did not simply stay there. It went up to the nape of her neck, and she turned away as if my touch tickled. Her eyes contained an ink-colored sky. Her white neck, slight breasts, slightly raised pink nipples. She blinked, and put her lips on my cheek. I would've trembled. And fit her dry lips to mine.

This is where the scene ends. And where it ends, there is no place where the minari grows, no girls with their clothes off. In its place is my bitter hurt and her cold disgust. As I put on the clothes I'd spread out on the grass, I thought: I will love you more than myself. But she must've thought the opposite. She never went back again to where the minari grows, and

*when I called for her or went to see her, she shouted so I'd be
scared away.*

*It was when spring passed and early summer was upon
us that finally I met her again on the bridge looking out over
the field. When I called her name, she fled. Then she turned
back, ran up to me, and punched the side of my face with all
her might. At the end of that soft joy, this pain . . .*

Her writing is blotted in places with tears.

*Where the minari grows, this scene I kept only to myself, her dry
lips, a soft joy, the deep green spot, I will love you more than myself—*
these are where the letters blur. She waits until the tears dry before
closing the notebook. And takes a sip of cooled coffee. The liquid
wets her chapped lips. She's trying to dredge up the motivation to
go back to the flower shop when her gaze suddenly rests on something outside the window. To her surprise, she sees the man. As the
tears on the page have been drying, the man has walked outside.
She recognizes him instantly. A woman stands next to him. There's
a camera bag hanging from his shoulder.

She puts one palm on the glass.

Just outside the café, the man stands at the crosswalk at the red
light, talking to the woman. He turns toward San at one point, send-
ing her heart into a beating frenzy. But the man does not see her.
His gaze travels over the café, over her face, registering nothing.

The light changes but the two do not cross.

The woman hands him her purse and book, and walks back
into the building.

On the other side of the window, San tenses as she stares at
the man. Her fixed stare pleads for him to recognize her. When
he does look she avoids his gaze, but not until he spots her face.
When he casts another nonchalant look into the café, she feels his
eyes settle on her face again. He sees as her cheeks turn red. But

he only passes over her once more. When the light changes, he moves closer to the building to avoid the wave of people crossing in his direction. She feels like she'll never breathe again. The man fails to recognize her.

It's because he fails to recognize her that she does the next thing.

San raises her head and stares directly at him. She calls desperately, I'm here. This feels intimate and she feels shy. How happy she would be if she could just say, It's me. If she could say to the man, instead of talking to herself, It's me.

The man outside looks bored.

He opens his camera bag and rummages, casting a backward glance at the building and lightly kicking the base of a tree growing by the road. He flexes his knees, nearly sitting down.

The devastation she felt earlier, when she closed her notebook, has disappeared. And while he brought on a spell of resentment just a moment ago, even that has dissipated. Just watching the man fidget makes her blush, in thrall at the sight. The woman comes back out. She takes back her purse and hands over a white envelope. She must have left the man on the street in order to fetch this envelope. The man takes it, doesn't check to see what's inside, and puts it into his bag.

The two face the far side of the street, ready to cross at the next green light. San's heart begins beating faster observing them. Her chair almost crashes into the table behind her but she's oblivious. Just as she's about to bolt out the door without paying, the server calls out, "Miss, miss, miss" three times before San turns around to face her. The server points at the cashier. San's body is already halfway out the door as she quickly pays. If the light changes, the man will cross the street and disappear. She wants to keep watch over him. That's the only thing on her mind right now.

But by the time she's paid, the man and woman have already crossed. They're going up the hill toward Samsung Hospital. Just as San steps off the curb, the light changes. A taxi, with its wheels poised over the painted line, honks and the driver leans out and shouts, "Are you crazy?"

Her eyes sorrowfully follow the couple.

That summer night, when she wore the plum-colored silk blouse, her goosebumps rising on her arm, and his calm words, *You must be cold*, the calm stroke of her arm, yes, that's when she began to desire him. What's strange is that in reality she hadn't been wearing a plum-colored silk blouse, but instead a white T-shirt for the farm, but her memory keeps insisting she wore the blouse.

Soon the light changes again and she crosses the street and bounds up the hill in a flash. The man and woman, at some distance from the main road, walk arm in arm. The man's lips occasionally hover by her earlobe. From behind, San blanches. Even as she nearly trips, the exertion of keeping them in sight makes her palms damp.

Where have they gone?

Once she's up the hill and past Samsung Hospital, she finds herself in an alley crowded with restaurants.

Pork belly and seafood stew, spiced cutlass fish, rice porridge — the signage is flashy and eye-catching but the man is nowhere to be seen. Her eyes have been staring intently but not actually seeing, widening as she looks this way and that. She follows every alley he might've gone down, but he's gone.

Where has he gone?

She begins to run.

Past the Jongnojang and Gommaru restaurants, a supermarket, and the weather station, she pants as she desperately looks for him. Gwanghwamun Studio. Completely out of breath, she stops in her tracks; she doesn't see him, and the road forks into two.

Hesitating between the straight path ahead and the one that splits off, she takes the path up to Gwanghwamun Studio because she can't see over the hill. Once she gets to the top and finds no trace of him, she hurries back down. Now she's at the point where the road splits in between Sajik Tunnel and Geumhwa Tunnel. She catches a glimpse of him just as he's going around Sajik Tunnel. She follows suit. Going up the path toward the library, the couple then walks down toward Sajik Park. On the hill, the foliage of the acacia trees flutters and casts shadows on the ground. The couple does not enter the park but travels down a side path. Far from the office, they now walk side by side, nearly stuck to each other. In front of them looms Inwangsan Mountain. They slowly walk up the hill before suddenly disappearing. San looks frantically about. In the distance, bathed in sunlight, there's an archery field, a dumpling merchant, an auto body shop, a travel agency, and the sign of an inn with a red tile roof. Underneath the summer sun, the trees cast their thick shadows on the mountain path leading up to Sajik Library and the Bugak Skyway, but the man she is looking for is not there.

The Silent Woods

San stands at the bus stop on her route back to the long room. The street is one she walks every day, but today the effort is unbearable. Walking from the flower shop to Gwanghwamun Plaza to the bus stop has exhausted her. The skin on one heel is peeling, and every time she steps on that foot, it's like sand rubbing into the open wound.

It's nine at night.

Where has she even walked?

She abandoned the roads leading to the mountains and walked the streets for hours, until a blister appeared on one heel. When she finally got back to the shop, Su-ae had already closed up for the day.

Light seeps out from a photography studio. It's called Lan and they specialize in family portraits. Passersby are drawn to the glow and stop to look at the displays. All of the photographed families are wearing good clothes and smiling. We're happy, they seem to say.

The bus stop is a little past the studio. While San waits, she tries to gather her thoughts by focusing on the museum, or on Café Palette, which is filled with armchairs.

A motorcycle comes to a stop in front of her.

"Where are you headed?"

She looks at the man sitting on the motorcycle. A policeman in uniform. He's parked right in front of her and grinning. A man with small eyes and a bulky body.

"I'm on patrol. I can take you where you're going if it's close."

He pats the seat. Two high school students waiting for the bus, talking on their phones and utterly uninterested in anything until now, only then look at San. They seem interested in what choice she will make.

"If it's on the way, get on."

San isn't hesitating; she simply does not understand what is going on. Perhaps intuiting good intentions from the policeman's eyes and smile, she finally hears him and tries to smile back. Her exhaustion brings her forehead to a frown despite her smiling lips.

"Get on."

The apartment is only two stops away by bus.

"Good, that's on the way of my rounds."

Under the nonplussed gaze of the students, San gets on the motorcycle, thinking it will only take a minute to go there.

"Hold on to me."

As soon as she gets on, the policeman speeds up. The exhaust in his wake briefly swirls the fallen ginkgo leaves.

Have they gone about a hundred meters?

The motorcycle comes to such an abrupt stop that she bumps her face against the policeman's back. She can smell his sweat right in her nose.

They pass streets lined with galleries and come to the three-way intersection by Jinseon Book Café where the traffic begins to slow down, and soon they come to a complete stop. She peels her face off his back and sits up straight. The policeman *tsk-tsks*. There's no space for even a motorcycle to wind its way through the buses, trucks, taxis, and cars. There are so many automobiles and no indication of when the traffic might move again. Wondering if it's a traffic light issue, San leans sideways and tries to look into the distance.

Suddenly, the motorcycle veers into a side street that leads up to Jeongdok Library.

"Where are we going?" she asks in surprise.

"We can't do anything about the traffic. But we can get to the road behind the Auditors' Building."

The road behind the Auditors' Building?

She's splashed with icy terror as she finally comes to her senses.

"Can you slow down?"

"Just grab my waist."

As the policeman drives into the side street, he increases his speed. Instinctively grabbing the man's waist, her grip grows tighter and tighter. Choi Wook-han Dentistry, Big Courtyard Restaurant, Yeh Artisans, Alley Snack Shop. She reads the signs, trying to determine where she is. In all the time she has lived here, she has never come across these streets. Groups of girls pass by, walking in threes and fours, watching San on the back of the motorcycle.

"Isn't this too much of a detour?"

"It's faster than walking."

The policeman supposedly on patrol says this like he's about to take her all the way to the apartment. Both sides of the streets are full of illegally parked cars. As the motorcycle speeds up, people walking in front of them duck between these cars. Some of them spit in their wake, shouting, You damn police!

When they get to a crossroads, the bike goes past Seonje Art Museum and makes a turn at Jeongdok Library into an unfamiliar street. A few boys, perhaps coming from the library, jump out of the way. This alley is lined with snack shops wafting the smell of ramen and fish-cake broth. As they pass the library, the street narrows. Leaves have fallen early here, and they tumble around in the empty alley.

"Just let me off here."

"Here?"

"Let me off."

"Wait a little. We're almost there."

How are these streets connected?

When they get out of the alley there's a bit of an incline, which leads onto a mountain path. Has there always been such an isolated path? Beyond the chain-link fences on either side are the woods. The trees stand silently in the darkness. Where are they?

The motorcycle increases speed as it goes uphill.

The faster they go, the more complicated her thoughts become. She can clearly remember newspaper headlines from a couple of months ago.

Motorcycle kidnappings on the rise. Motorcycle gangs infiltrate residential areas. Around 9 p.m. last night, Miss Hong (anon), a word processor operator coming home from work, was kidnapped not fifty meters away from her home, taken to a playground, and assaulted. She was discovered much later and died on her way to the hospital.

The night city below whips by between the trees.

Aside from the noise of the motorcycle, she feels no sound or presence in the forest. She tries hard to calm herself and grips tighter at the policeman's clothing.

The trees beyond the fence look like spectators.

By the road stands a bench totally oblivious to the scene. To think that such a road exists in the middle of the city. When the incline ends and the mountain road levels out a bit, the policeman drastically decreases his speed. She bumps her face against his back again.

"The city at night looks nice; shall we take a look?"

He's switched to an informal register.

San breaks into a sweat. How did I get myself in this mess? She can't understand her behavior at the bus stop. Why did she get on a motorcycle with a stranger at the drop of a hat? Did his uniform make her complacent? Her fatigue has evaporated.

The policeman takes one foot off the pedal and steps on the mountain road.

Mother!

In her mind, she finds herself calling out for her mother. Please help me, mother. Her fear is so intense, to the point of passing into calm. Now she's fallen back to the San who existed before seeing the photographer through the café windows, to the rational woman she was before being led around by a hallucination.

"Let's take a walk."

San has to do whatever it takes to get down off this mountain path. She can't get off the motorcycle until then. Bracing herself, she grips the man's clothes even harder.

"Sir, let's just go." Trying not to let on that she's nervous, she adds a bit of a flirtatious whine in her voice and puts a smile on her face. "I mean, it's a great view. I had no idea there was such a view of Seoul here. But I've got to come back some other time. I'm kind of cold right now and coming down with something. I think I need some hot tea at home."

"You're feeling sick?"

"Yes."

"You live alone?"

"Yes." Thinking of Su-ae, she agrees the second time with emphasis.

All she can think about right now is keeping this policeman in the dark. That she cannot afford to make him angry. That she has to get him to take her off this mountain.

"Oh wait!" She grips his waist again. As if remembering something, she suggests, "Sir, you simply must come to my room and have some tea—I just got some new leaves from Jirisan Mountain. You've done so much for me, it's the least I can do. And I get to try my new tea."

She's made her voice breathy, almost juvenile, but the policeman doesn't answer. She pulls him a bit closer to her and whispers, "Come on, sir, let's go."

The policeman still doesn't answer.

"My room is just down this road."

"But the view," he insists. "You don't see that every day."

San protests softly.

"Let's just get off for a moment first."

To think she got on to this motorcycle just because he was a policeman! If anything, policemen were more dangerous. No. She tries to calm her panic. This policeman is not doing this deliberately. He really was just patrolling. The only bus that passes that way is the 104 and so he knows it ends at Samcheong-dong, that it was only two stations away, and she keeps trying to convince herself he has good intentions—she just about manages to contain her panic. The skyline has truly caught his interest for a moment, that's all.

Through the silent darkness, a pair of headlights slowly approaches the motorcycle. Is it lovers who have been parked nearby? As the car's headlights beam and illuminate the two, the policeman, who was about to dismount, starts his engine once more. The cool night air slams against her face.

She holds on tight to the policeman's waist.

The car and motorcycle zoom past each other.

"Are you really going to make me a cup of tea at home?"

"Of course."

Her voice is bright, but her face is grimacing behind his back.

As the motorcycle winds through the mountain road, she sees the familiar sight of Samcheong Park and the street that splits below it. How did that previous silent and empty road connect? She lets out an involuntary sigh of relief. With it, the tension leaves her body.

"Let me off."

She sees lights now, and people passing by. Cars are lined up in the parking lot. Restaurants with shabby signage have their lights on, reassuring her.

"Let me off."

"What's wrong with you, lady?"

"Let me off, now!"

It could get awkward for him if she starts to scream on the back of the motorcycle. He comes to a stop at the top of the hill. When she gets off, the policeman increases his speed and zips away down the road.

As soon as the motorcycle disappears, she collapses onto the road. Passersby stare. A high school student walking by comes up and asks, "Are you okay?" She offers San her water bottle. San takes it and gulps down the water with her mouth on the spout. When she tries to hand it back, the young girl grins. The bottle is empty.

"I'm sorry."

The girl says, "That's all right," and then adds, "Do you need help?"

As San heaves herself up with some effort, the student lets San lean on her as they carefully make their way to a public phone booth. Once she sees San putting coins into the phone, the girl finally goes on her way.

After the phone rings three or four times and she hears Su-ae's voice, she feels her knees buckle.

"Can you come and get me?"

"What's wrong? What happened?"

"I'm at the phone booth in front of Samcheong Park."

Su-ae cuts off her own questions, says, "I'll be there in a second," and hangs up.

Is it five minutes later?

Having run through the dark, Su-ae finds San sitting inside the telephone booth and stares as if she doesn't quite register the scene. This is the same path where they would go to get water from the spring. Not even bothering to ask what's going on, Su-ae tries to get San up on her feet. No matter what she does, San simply falls back down like a scarecrow. She doesn't have the strength to stay upright. Su-ae tries to carry her on her back but, being smaller than San, she can't manage her weight.

Su-ae darts to a man in the parking lot about to start his car. The apartment is only five minutes away by foot, but Su-ae can't think of any other way to bring San back. In the dark, San wearily watches Su-ae talking through the man's driver's side window, both of them looking at her. The car drives up and the door opens. Su-ae supports her as San gets into the backseat.

"Thank you so much," Su-ae says when they're finally going up to the apartment, and she holds San up by the waist. The landlady, who has since returned, sees them struggling.

"Is she sick?"

Supported by Su-ae, San really does look like a patient. When they don't answer her, the landlady gives them one last look before going inside. They go upstairs.

"What happened?"

Su-ae has been patient, not asking any questions until they reached the long room, and now it's as if she's berating San.

"Can I have some water?"

An inexplicable thirst ambushes San. Her esophagus will burn if she doesn't have water. Even after Su-ae pours her three glasses, it doesn't quench San's thirst.

Her chapped lips are split and slightly bloodied.

After downing more water, she lies down and screws her eyes shut. Determined to get to the bottom of things, Su-ae stands by and waits for San to open her eyes. When she does, Su-ae asks outright, "What's going on?"

As soon as San finishes telling her about how she got on the motorcycle at the bus stop and went up the mountain road and then escaped, Su-ae launches into a tirade.

"What is wrong with you? Do you have any idea what kind of danger you were in? And how incredible that with all that stupidity, you managed to stay on that motorcycle! This guy isn't just any person, he's a cop! Plus, he knows you took a good look at his face; he's not going to let you get away this easily!"

Once finished, Su-ae manages to ask, "You saw his face, right? You can recognize him, right?"

San confirms, "Yes."

Su-ae calls a few people, after which she mumbles, "Yes, I suppose he could just say he gave her a ride with good intentions," and then covers San with a blanket to let her rest. But she slams the door as she leaves the room, as if she can't contain her rage.

The city is asleep. Perhaps it's about to be dawn.

San sits up in the darkness of the long room. Su-ae, who had returned at some point in the night, is sleeping. The herbs and carnivorous Venus flytrap sit and stare at her. The standoff on the mountain road rises and falls in her mind, over and over. Lying down, lying on her stomach, nothing seems to work. Her head hurts and she feels acid in her throat; she can't remain supine anymore. The Venus flytrap, which uses the long room as its greenhouse, grows fatter by the day eating the kinds of bugs that stick to the window screen.

San gets to her feet, picking up her bag and opening the door quietly so as not to wake her roommate, treading lightly as she walks down the stairs. She closes the door and is passing the outer wall of the Prime Minister's office when she almost trips over the edge of the pavement. There she is, suppressing the shout that nearly explodes from her body, and there she is, slowly walking again. Cold air whirls around her neck and calves. The occasional cab passes, but she ignores them as she walks the empty city streets underneath the canopy of ginkgo leaves. When she reaches the flower shop, she raises the shutters and turns on the lights near the entrance.

A familiar scent has crowded the darkness. The frown on her forehead smooths away as soon as she smells it. She breathes in the fragrance deeply. Putting her bag down, she turns on all the lights.

The gloxinias and lilies of the valley, the gardenias that so resemble the hot summer sun—they've all been replaced by fall flowers. The scarlet West Indian jasmines, the orange lantanas, and the gentians erupting into purple trumpets. The wild Indian chrysanthemums have little golden blossoms coming in at the ends of their stems. Heavy in the buckets are the white asters, shoved into the narrow corridors.

She pulls up a chair and sits down among the green plants, stacked in double, triple layers.

How much time has passed?

She slowly gets up from the chair and turns off the lights.

It's dark inside the flower shop.

Sitting in the darkness, she begins to weep. Softly at first, but soon her sobs grow more violent.

In a single moment, after a summer of nothing happening, an old and intense desire has flooded her body from the depths of her heart. This free fall for a man she didn't even know inflamed old, anxious feelings, which had previously been dulled and mitigated by tending the plants. When she found herself awake in the middle of the night, she would return to the flower shop despite her overwhelming fatigue. She would compulsively push the plants' roots into the soil and their stems into the air. But now crying engulfs her.

This desire grew slowly, stronger and stronger, but it never had any place to escape except for into sorrow. It has caused her to choose neglect. It has refused to be sublimated, but instead reappeared as a fresh green sadness. San's attraction did not originate this summer, but rather, it has lain in wait for millennia before bursting forth all at once. Holding that desire to her breast, her earlobes red with heat, she cries long and hard inside the flower shop.

I wonder: Is this your first time hearing this cry? This cry, which for centuries was never given an ear, or a means to be heard?

Nun

San stands before the elementary school she attended as a child. Her hair has been cut short. Despite rarely wearing makeup, she now sports violet eyeshadow and her cheeks have been rouged. She looks like a different person. The first thing she did when she got off the train was to enter a hair salon. The small-town hairdresser's skills were not the best. Her hairstyle doesn't look natural and there are blunt lines cut into the sides and back. But the hairdresser seemed to believe in her own work. What do you think? Isn't this a wonderful change? She even shaved off San's eyebrows and drew in new ones. San, staring at her reflection, said nothing as the hairdresser added eyeshadow and rouge.

In her memory, there's an Episcopal church on the way to the elementary school, and past that, a stationery store. And perhaps the store has a pair of geese out front. She wanders through the five-way and four-way hubs of the town's market and alleys, asking for directions here and there, until finally she arrives at the elementary school. From about a hundred meters before the gate, she sees high-rise apartment buildings, making her hesitate and wonder, Am I in the right place? The houses with low slate roofs have disappeared. The hill behind the school has also disappeared, replaced with another phalanx of apartment buildings, and the school is effectively now surrounded. Before, they had to brave the ire of two geese and their yellow beaks if they wanted to make it to school.

As if searching for the geese, she watches the stationery store from outside the gate.

Poplars grow right up to the sky. A swing set, and a slide next to that. When her gaze reaches the red brick of the school building, it finally feels like she's in the right place. Aside from a new building next to the teachers' office, everything, even the water fountain, is the same. Maybe a couple of new statues planted here and there.

Class must be in session, as the playground is empty and silent.

There's the raised stage where the principal would stand on Mondays and give an assembly speech. The wind makes the poplars lining the path from the front to back gate flutter their leaves. She stares up at where she had her fourth and fifth grade classes but doesn't go in. At the stationery store, a middle-aged woman pokes out her head and looks at the back of the woman standing awkwardly by the gate. The geese are no more.

San slips into the alley next to the stationery store. It's a short-cut to her village.

Is it still populated by the Yis? Who owned all that farmland and the forest? Aunts, uncles, cousins, and in-laws to each other.

Is Namae still there?

If Namae had left the village, she would've heard of it, San thinks. And if she has, then at the very least, San can learn where Namae went. And once she does, she is going to see her. Just once. After San left for the town, and then moved on to Suwon, she never went back to the village, not even once. But her steps are taking her there now. The alley that used to be just wide enough for three children to walk side by side, or for one bicycle to run through, is now paved over and big enough to be a street. If she had not seen the gateless old house at the end, she would not have thought this was the same alley. Turning at that house will bring her onto the country road.

It was an old house, but it always bustled with children.

Seen from the road, there was always someone eating dinner on the porch, or bringing up water from the well, or hanging laundry. Right next to the house there was a terraced paddy. Doubt crosses San's face as if she wonders if this is indeed the right place. The terraced paddies have disappeared, giving way to apartment buildings that spill over from behind the school.

She stares into the house, returning to old habits.

It has the structure of a house, but no one seems to be living there. There's a miasma of ruin about it. A couple of sparrows sit on the laundry lines crossing the courtyard, before flitting away at her footsteps. She tries to remember where the well was, where she would plunge in a gourd for a drink, thirsty on her walk home.

Was it over there?

She steps into the courtyard of the ruined house as if pushed. Looking back, she walks toward the spot where she remembers the well. Behind her are the tall apartments that have taken over the terraced paddy. The house looks long abandoned. The ground by the well is completely dry, rocks and stones scattered about, straw and leaves blown in by the wind.

There are no people here. Only the well stands guard.

Holding her breath, she balances her elbows on the edge and looks inside. Still black water. A little piece of sky. Sky over black water—at first the image makes her heart hurt, but then she sees her own face. She shakes her head. The face in the black water shakes its head too. Completely still, she stares as if to pierce the water with her gaze. The face stares back at her in return. A chill goes down her spine. Having been pushed by something into the house, she now feels as if she's being pushed back out again. She flees the old house with the well, making such haste that she almost trips over her own feet. Walking so fast she's soon out of breath, she finds herself at the main road once more.

The village seemed a mountain away, but the mountain she'd

have to climb is gone. There was a bridge to cross before climbing that mountain, but the bridge is gone too. The acacia forest past the bridge—now no more. All the twisted, dusty roads where the children would bet on who could race the fastest, or who could dig up mud first, it's all disappeared. Before her instead is a straight asphalt road.

Is it still here?

Namae's mother's grave.

The girl, whose father would get drunk and climb into the jar to sing, would put her ear to that grave, along with San. Despite the unfamiliar surroundings, San still recognizes the grave, overgrown with weeds, discarded between the rice paddy and the field below. Another grave has appeared next to it. When she makes her way down the dike, the tall weeds whip about her calves. They hurt. She tries to avoid the fleabanes, leechworts, and columbines, but they're simply too thick. Her hair falls into her eyes. She smiles bitterly in front of the graves. She remembers carrying everyone's backpacks with Namae, like two wandering pilgrims, and Namae asking her, *Why don't you walk ahead of me like everyone else?* Memories swirl past her and her throbbing calves. Namae's voice saying, *I lost, why are you asking to share the bags? Do you like me? Why? Why do you like me?* San whispers with dry lips, "I hope someday I'll be able to explain, like this, how you managed to take my heart." San puts down her bag, gets up on the grave, and lies down flat. Adjusting her position, she puts her ear to it as if listening carefully. As if desperate to hear something.

How much time has passed?

Coming down from the grave, she picks up her bag and quickens her step.

Is Namae still there? In that village where the wild minari grew around the southern dike? The asphalt continues all the way there and beyond. Houses previously connected by dirt now have this asphalt. The only things on the road are the shadows of the persimmon trees; the village is like a ghost town. She stares at the houses for a while and looks about for the minari field. The minari, which might have predated the village, is nowhere to be found; there are only the straight, even divides of rice paddies. The yellow of the ripening grain fills her sight.

She looks left and right, searching.

When the minari would rise from the mud in the spring, the entire village would look as if it were hugging a grassy plain. After its distinct fragrance had disappeared for the winter, villagers would sprinkle compost or chicken droppings on the ground. Past July and around August, the minari would explode into white flowers, and it would look like fallen snow. The wind passing through the blossoms brought to mind tinkling bells. When the field had thickened enough, people from other villages would come in their boots and snap off stems. Despite occasionally falling prey to leeches, they would be glad to harvest their portion. And on the table of many a first birthday feast, long stems of stir-fried minari would wish the baby a long life.

Mother, who ripped up fresh minari to drop into kimchi.

Mother, who made a tea of crushed minari when San came home with a fever.

Where has everyone gone?

San pushes open the gate to the house where her mother, after becoming the first divorced woman in the village, rented a small room. Clotheslines are heavy with white laundry. Thousands of green jujubes shine on a tree near the wall. There are so many jujubes that a pole props up one of the heavy branches. It's the same for the quince tree nearby. There's so much fruit that the branches curve downward. Thinking she might bump into someone, she looks in on some other houses, but there's no one in any of them. A crouching dog near a porch looks at her but doesn't bark.

Giving up, she walks toward the new village.

San's steps are unhurried, like those on the days her mother and grandmother fought, or whenever Namae wasn't around and she would walk toward the field. She would sit on that dike alone, even when the minari was gone and there was only the swamp left. The house she was born in at the end of the new village is completely gone; in its place is a warehouse. It's not only her house that has been knocked down but the neighbor's as well; the warehouse sits across both lots. Waving cosmos surround the warehouse, and an arching overpass has been built over the train tracks. Now that there is an overpass, there is no reason for the guardhouse—which was charged with lowering the crossing gate across the tracks—to exist anymore, but she looks underneath the overpass anyway. She remembers the gate lowering when a train passed, its operator saluting until it disappeared.

She turns around from the warehouse.

Does Namae's house still exist?

That frightful day when her mother's scissors were ready to fly toward her grandmother's face. The day she found the tension unbearable and ran out of the house alone and rubbed her forehead against the wall the persimmon tree had grown over. She kept thinking as she ran toward the field: I wish I could run away as far as possible. Even better, she had thought, if she never had to come back.

But here she was, having come back—a strange smile spreads across her face. As she thinks the house should be near, her eyes suddenly brighten. Namae's house is still the same: blue door, low wall, the roof with the bad tile work.

She pushes the gate and peers inside.

Large earthen jars along the garden wall. A well. The space beneath the porch.

All the roads have changed and the house she was born in has been replaced by a warehouse, but Namae's house looks as if time has stood still. The pomegranate tree is still there, and the wooden door leading to the kitchen. She is slightly disconcerted by how little Namae's house has changed. How can it look so exactly the same?

She can almost see the severed chicken head in the corner of the yard. Namae, who hugged the body and rolled about on the ground. The dusk, the splatters of blood on the jars, the wall, the well. Namae, stumbling backward, screaming, climbing onto the porch with her shoes on, running into one of the rooms and locking the door behind her.

San pushes open the gate and steps onto the lawn.

"Namae-yah!"

Unlike her previous hesitation, she walks eagerly toward the house and looks about for signs of life. But her voice echoes in the emptiness. Not even an ant crawls past. Whether because she's listening carefully or because the silence is too much to bear, she keeps calling out, "Namae-yah," and walks right up to the porch. It feels like someone might open one of the doors at any moment, but there is still no sign of life. There she stands, calling out, "Namae-yah," one more time.

"Who are you?"

This question comes not from the house but from the road. Turning around, San sees a woman wearing a loose shirt with baggy chestnut-colored trousers and a straw hat. Wondering if she's trespassed too far into someone's house, San comes back out the gate.

Is the woman pregnant? The front of her checkered shirt protrudes roundly.

"No one is in right now. Who are you looking for?"

"Isn't this Namae's house?"

"Namae isn't here."

"Where did she go?"

"Who is asking?"

San is tongue-tied before lowering her head and answering, "I'm a friend of Namae's."

The woman nods in acceptance and gestures, repeating, "No one is in right now."

"Where can I go to see Namae?"

"Namae left the village after her father passed."

The woman winces as if in pain and rests her hand on the small of her back. She looks to turn away.

"Where did she go?"

"I don't know."

There are brown freckles underneath the woman's eyes. She's about to say something but closes her mouth once more. Fidgeting with her straw hat, she makes again to leave.

"Who can I ask if I want to know where Namae has gone?"

"Well, Namae's aunt is probably at the mountain patches; she's the one who lives in this house now."

"How do I get to the mountain patches?"

"If you go toward Yeosulan it'll be on the road."

"Yeosulan?"

The woman, who seems to find it difficult to stay on her feet, manages to describe the way to Yeosulan and turns her back on San's goodbye. Following her directions, San passes the warehouse where her house used to be. She stares as if it's grand and imposing, and then hurries past. The uphill path toward the mountain patches is crowded with threatening cosmos, entangling her ankles. Their mixed white, pink, and scarlet blossoms dance in the wind. Behind the cosmos are thick flailing reeds, eager to slap her face. She avoids the cosmos and reeds. But even the autumn light rakes down her face. The wild plants here are hostile. Past the graves, the paddies are filled with panicles on the cusp of ripening. The rice is ready to lunge at her.

In the mountain patches is a bent-over woman with a towel

wrapped around her head. On nearby stalks dangle a few shriveled or bug-eaten chili peppers. Without being sure that this
is Namae's aunt, San desperately stumbles toward her. The
rippling vines wrap around her limbs, the dried chili stalks are
like rods slapping her arms. Her forehead is soaked in sweat.
The woman snaps sprouts from the sweet potato vines and
drops them in the basket next to her; she looks up once or twice
at San and seems to wonder, Who is that, presently stopping
her work.

As San makes her way to the woman, the sweet potato planted
on the mountainside shifts to look like minari. The mirage causes
a memory to rise up like the tide. A girl with a narrow ridge of a
nose . . . We started by taking off our shoes and putting them on
the dike and splashing each other. The sediment from the bottom
made the water murky, and the waterweeds got tangled and danced.
You almost fell, but then you righted yourself, and your lips turned
blue as ink, black pupils, the braid that came down to your little
shoulders, your small cheeks. A girl with a green grass stain on
her back. How softly that stain wrapped you; it made me stretch
out my hand to put my palm to it when our eyes met and yours
went wide with surprise, and your hurt voice. You were close to
tears because you were so angry at your spot being revealed. You
sobbed that you hadn't wanted to show it to anyone. How beautiful it was, I thought. How could it have been so silent around us?
The roads were empty. The dikes were, too. Only the green minari
was rippling and swaying like waves.

San stops in her tracks and places her hands on her back. The
colorful, unruly chrysanthemums scream at her. She finds it hard
to breathe in front of these wildflowers and weeds. The very trees
and grasses harbor animosity. Just one misstep will trip her ankles
or slap her cheek.

How you would curl your body and caress your anklebone.

The feeling of hugging Namae's back revives itself in San's memory. The moment when their flesh touched, skin warmed by the sun, was maybe when San's loneliness had been born. In that moment, when San and Namae awkwardly held each other and looked into each other's eyes.

The woman in the patch is still wondering who she is. The sweet potato leaf sprouts are still in her hand.

The wind that used to blow past the railway tracks and dike and chili pepper stalks now weaves through the mountain patch.

"Who are you?" asks the woman with the rust-colored towel on her head as San approaches. Behind the woman, the reeds on the dike are shaking, and beyond that, far off in the distance, are the railroad tracks.

"Are you Namae's aunt?"

"I am."

San avoids the nakai and goldenrod and tangles of squash flowers as she approaches.

"And who are you, young lady?"

"I'm a friend of Namae's."

The woman peers intently. Again the wind passes, and as the sprouts lean on one side and dance, the woman finally stands up.

"Are you not San? Who lived in the new village?"

Unexpectedly, San is recognized.

"I would never have recognized you on the street!"

She clasps San's hands. Namae's aunt, whose hands are rough from working in the fields and rice paddies—San has no recollection of her face. Since her welcome greeting provokes no response from San, the woman gently drops San's hands and mumbles, "How strange that is. You know, your mother came here last spring."

Mother.

"She was looking for you here."

San says nothing.

"Neither of you ever visited once after you left, but here are mother and daughter, coming back in the spring and fall of the same year. Has something happened?"

". . ."

"Your mother was very sick. Is she better now? She could barely walk, that one."

Over the patch and the reeds and the rice paddies runs a clanking train headed to either Gwangju or Mokpo. When it's passed, the woman sits down again and continues to tug at the sweet potato sprouts, placing them in the basket.

"Where is Namae?"

At San's inquiry, the aunt stops snapping leaf sprouts and peers at her again.

"The year she graduated high school, she said she would become a nun and has never been back."

A nun.

San hears a great roaring in her ears as if she's standing next to a waterfall. Namae became a nun? Speechless, all she can do is stand still and stare.

San returned to the village to avoid the desire to see her mother in Suwon. She left the flower shop in the morning, bought a train ticket, and has rifled through her memories to make her way back here, only to learn that Namae has become a nun. When her train passed Suwon, she bowed her head so she wouldn't even see any signs bearing the name.

"Why on earth did you even come back here? All you did here was suffer because of your father. It's not like you have any relations here."

"You don't have Namae's address?"

"She could be dead for all I know, poor thing."

Namae's aunt says, "That's it for today," as if San had been working alongside her, gets up, dusts herself off, hoists the basket to her side, and leads the way. Still feeling threatened by the purslanes, reeds, and bedstraws, San follows.

"That was your house, wasn't it?"

When they're near the new village, Namae's aunt points out the warehouse and tosses out the question. San's blank stare conveys her fatigue. The skin beneath her eyes is turning blue.

"And the minari field?"

"What minari field? All that's in the past now."

She suspected the minari field was no more after seeing her childhood home gone, but the confirmation fills her heart with despair.

Namae's aunt passes some houses with old slate roofs. The new village looks empty. There's an abandoned cultivator at the embankment. They pass the ditch and the hackberry tree. Orange-colored berries hang off the green hackberry branches. San strokes her cheeks with her two hands. The berries are poised to fly at her.

Pausing before a rice paddy, Namae's aunt points out a different, faraway plot.

"That used to be the minari field."

San stares out at where she points. There's no evidence of the vast minari field. Just rice ripening underneath the autumn sunlight. Have even the dikes been rebuilt? She can't see the ditch.

"They spent years straightening these fields. All that minari turned into neat rectangles."

The aunt mumbles nonchalantly. San reaches for one of the rice tassels and tugs at it. The stalk springs back, supple. No villagers in sight; there's only the paddies. A fleeting memory of the man causes her heart to squeeze momentarily. As she recalls his face, the village's trees—acacias, oaks, and pines—rustle like they might charge at the slightest provocation. Her gaze shakes as they look up at the mountains. Wild brambles creep up around her feet, up to her neck. She waves her hands, trying to cast off the vines entangling her. The man has to be kept locked away in her heart, but he must never be approached. Not because he's a womanizer or because he's of a different class. He must never be approached because of that overwhelming *thing* that made her mount a stranger's motorcycle the other night, negligent of her own safety: the burning loneliness soaring up from within her subconscious, ever since Namae threw her aside. Through the years that loneliness took root inside her, and whenever she tried to approach anyone, it screamed, Get away, get away.

I have to go back, she thinks.

She left the shop at dawn and visited not her mother but this village because of the words eating through her heart, desperately searching for Namae. If she could just see Namae, that twisting and turning inside her chest might finally burst through. And if she could spill out these words, then maybe her other desire might also be satiated. But there is nothing left in the village. Not the house she was born in, not where the wild minari grew—not even Namae.

"Goodbye."

As she bows to Namae's aunt, the latter looks concernedly at San's chapped lips. She grabs San's arm.

"Why don't you have dinner before you go?"

". . ."

"If I knew she would never call or visit, I would've given her another warm meal before she left. It's just like having Namae back. And you know it isn't our way to send off visitors without a proper meal."

Namae's aunt, basket wedged under one arm, walks toward the house. The late afternoon sunlight lingers. When the aunt realizes San is just standing there, she turns and gestures for her to follow. Feeling trapped, San starts to walk, whereupon the aunt turns and goes her way again. San can see the roofs of the village, the hackberry tree, and the narrow alley leading to the main road. Until they reach the empty house, Namae's aunt walks in front and she follows behind. Their distance narrows not a bit. Not knowing that San already hesitated in front of Namae's house earlier that day, the aunt stops until San catches up. She says, "This was Namae's house. I live here now. Do you remember?"

Inside the gate, San looks again at the jars standing along the wall. The aunt puts down her basket and bustles into the kitchen. After an uncertain moment, San follows her in. From the outside, the house is unchanged, but the kitchen has been remodeled. There's a gas range in place of the fuel hole and a sink where the water jar used to be. There are mounted shelves with neatly lined spices. A pair of pink rubber gloves hang over the sink and a few black plastic bags roll about the floor. The aunt, coming back with a bowl of uncooked rice, sees San folding up the plastic bags and tells her to wash her hands at the well and wait inside the house. San must be tired, but could she gather the laundry?

Turning away from the glare of the pomegranate tree, San washes her hands and wipes her hands on a towel hanging on the clothesline. She grabs the laundry, takes her shoes off, and walks into the house. Folding the blue shirt, two pairs of pink-and-white socks, and two towels, she pushes them aside and leans against the wall. All the kitchen noise comes through.

The sound of rice being washed, water being run, the rice cooker lid opening, footsteps. After a moment of silence, there's the rhythmic sound of chopping. Garlic being crushed with a knife, a rag being squeezed, a spoon falling on the floor. These sounds rend her heart, and she moves away from the wall. It was on mornings when she would leave that her mother would make such busy kitchen noises. White rice and seaweed soup and fleshy croaker. Her mother was going to abandon her again. San quietly opens the door, picks up her bag, and slides her feet into her shoes. Without saying goodbye to Namae's aunt, still cooking in the kitchen, she leaves through the front gate. Once she's outside, she hurries to the road as if chased.

When she reaches the street, her expression becomes disconcerted. Perhaps too anxious to wait for the bus, she instead makes her way, quickly, toward the town. This is not her exhausted walk at the disappeared minari field; it's a determined one, to escape and leave the village behind. With movements more deliberate than any she has made before, she walks rapidly across the bridge leaving the village, and never once looks back.

Only when she hears the bus behind her does she pause.

Despite the fact that it's not a stop, she hails it. The bus looks like it's going to pass but ends up stopping. Gripping the strap of her bag, she jumps on.

Is it because it's almost sunset?

Aside from an old man in the very back, it's empty. She collapses into the seat right behind the driver. He gives her a look through the rearview mirror. Sighing, she finally turns to look back at the village just as they turn onto the mountain roads.

Now she stands at the train station.

Looking up the train times, she takes out some cash, pushes it through the slot of the ticketing office, and asks for Seoul. Ticket in hand, she waits in the reception area for forty minutes, head bowed and not moving at all, until the announcement is made for her train. She drags herself to her feet, walks through the gates and down the steps to an underground passage, and comes up on the correct platform. There are empty chairs but she doesn't sit in them. Seven minutes later, a train from Yeosu pulls in, and she boards. As soon as she gets in her seat, sleep overtakes her. San falls so deeply asleep that it seems she'll never surface again.

I Went to the Beach

San stands in front of the flower shop late at night.

She raises the shutters, unlocks the door, and enters. Without turning on the lights, she puts her bag down on the table and falls into the chair. Even though she slept the whole time on the train, and despite the discomfort of being slumped over the desk, she again drifts into a sleep so deep it's like sinking into a swamp.

A nightmare. Vines wrapping around her neck—she opens her eyes and her hands touch her throat. Where am I, she thinks. The eerie darkness and the shallow breathing of the plants make her realize she is in the flower shop. Sighing with relief, she straightens her back. She gets up and switches on the lights. The plants, now illuminated, glare at her.

Is she going to open the shop early? She unlocks the door and raises the shutters. Stacked in the corridor are the sago palms and weeping figs that she pushes away. Trying to ignore the feeling that they're about to attack her, she puts the little pots with cobalt gentians outside. She raises the display rack and puts it next to the gentians, arranging the Indian chrysanthemums and white bog star on top of it. A tremor of fear passes through her. The plants, that had always felt friendly, now feel—from the gentians and bog stars to the yellow chrysanthemums with their little hairs—as if they're piercing her every time she touches them. She looks up from her bustling and stares at the shiny asters lounging in the blue buckets. She's never seen them before. Su-ae must've brought them from the Gupabal farm. The thick leaves with their white, neat flowers look as if they're about to hurl themselves over the bucket to strangle her. She takes the asters out, pours out the water, fills the bucket with fresh water, and puts the asters back. The smile she used to have when handling flowers is gone.

It's early dawn, and a few pedestrians roam outside.

Why in the world is a flower shop open at this hour, some of them seem to think, peering inside as they hurriedly pass by. When Paris Baguette opens, selling bread and soup for breakfast, San crosses the street to buy milk and a pastry. Just when she's poured herself a cup, Su-ae charges into the shop.

Her rage is so palpable that San lowers the milk glass.

Su-ae stares at her haircut and seems about to say something when instead she stomps to the back of the shop and returns, changed out of her checkered skirt and into her baggy work khakis. Not even so much as looking at San, who has put down her glass and offers no excuse. Su-ae gathers peat moss and a pair of pincers to divide the Dendrobium orchid roots. She brings out support rods and sits down in the legless chair deep inside the flower shop. Turning the pot, she knocks it along the side until the plant is loose enough to be pulled out. She snips off the roots' rotten ends without giving San a second glance. She moves on to pinching off the dying blossoms, concentrating hard on her work.

San stands behind Su-ae.

Previously, Su-ae would've lectured about how in order to see beautiful flowers, one must be true to the roots, that plants need plenty of sun and wind, that while they love water, keeping them soaked is bad for them, that watering them sometimes keeps them from forming buds. But now, silent, she expertly snips off the rotten ends, arranges the remaining roots, and carefully divides the individuals so as not to damage them. San places some moss close by so Su-ae can easily reach it, but Su-ae takes moss from farther away and divides it in half before wrapping the roots. She seems determined to ignore the person right next to her. She plants the orchids in another pot, presses down firmly on the peat moss, sticks in a supporting rod, and winds wires around the stems, not once looking at San.

"I went to the beach."

Su-ae stares at San.

"I went by train and then by bus. No. Maybe it wasn't the beach. It was a place where red flowers bloomed everywhere. No. It was the beach. A vast beach with white, firm sand. The sand was rough, and there was a long and white table, the planks rough to the touch but solid, right in front of the blue ocean. You would have been surprised if you saw it, too. It was the firmest and most beautiful table I'd ever seen."

What is she trying to say?

Watering the divided orchids, Su-ae brings the two pots out to the rack San had placed outside, and only then does she look at San's sunken face. She's never heard San say so many words at once.

"I picked some flowers and decorated the four corners of the desk. I spent all day atop this desk by the sea. You don't know how free I felt. Like the chains around me were melting. A group of little girls who lived in the seaside village also came and played with me. People passing by would take my flowers and leave food in their place. So I was never hungry. I don't know for how many days I lived like that. I fell asleep, but when I woke up, the little girls had all gone back and I was by myself with the desk floating in the middle of the ocean. How strange that was. I was not scared at all. The ocean water was so gentle. The wind kept blowing, and the waves would tickle my hands and feet. Occasionally a wave would wrap itself around my waist and hug me. I could feel the seawater entering my ears and eyes. But I wasn't scared. The ocean water was carrying me on that firm and beautiful desk to a faraway land."

As she listens to San's mumbling, Su-ae gets up and fishes out a cigarette and lighter from her bag. San, who seems like she would have continued, shuts her mouth. Su-ae would never normally smoke inside the shop, but she puts a cigarette to her mouth and lights it.

"Hey!"

As Su-ae breathes out smoke, San's vacant eyes start to tremble. Why has she shaved her eyebrows? Su-ae stares at how different her friend looks.

"Are you all right?"

San says nothing.

"Well, are you?"

"Yes."

"Where did you go yesterday?"

" . . . "

"Did you go to the beach?"

San shakes her head.

"Then where?"

" . . . "

"Where were you all day?"

"Sorry. I have to quit my job here."

Su-ae throws her cigarette onto the ground. It hits the wet floor with a hiss. She grabs her bag and leaves, slamming the door so hard that it cracks.

She doesn't come back even past lunchtime. San sells some asters, takes orders for twenty lucky bamboos, and occasionally looks out into the street wondering if Su-ae will return. The cars and pedestrians cast shadows in the fully ripe sun. On the side of the Sejong Arts Center is a poster for an opera performance. She stares at the empty telephone booth and then turns her gaze back toward the Gwanghwamun side. Su-ae isn't there.

Just as lunch ends, there's a call from the Gupabal farm. The youth who works there says the farm owner is asking whether all is well at the shop. She says, Yes. The youth asks to speak to Su-ae. The farm owner has something he needs to say. She hesitates when the youth relays the information that Su-ae was very angry the other day and the farm owner wonders if San knows something. The youth must be reading what the farm owner has written. "He says you should try to get along with Su-ae. He's never seen her take to someone like she's taken to you."

As the youth is about to hang up, San says, "Wait—"

The youth answers, "What is it?"

"Are the ficus growing well?"

She wanted to tell the farm owner she was quitting, but she ends up asking that instead. The youth, after a moment of tension, laughs.

"Of course. They're growing very well. Come see them sometime."

The youth pauses to see if she has anything more to add and then says, "All right," and hangs up. The Gupabal farm and the stream where the ficus stand in lines. The wind that makes their green leaves flutter in one direction. The prowling pregnant cat. A scar ruining its face, dumped in a sack and driven past Jayu motorway and Ilsan into Tongil Dongsan where it was thrown out under a bridge, but somehow found its way back. The papaya palms accidentally smuggled in. Identical side by side, sprouting seven leaves each, fresh as little boys. *It's amazing! Two seeds, growing into this. And they're all alone here, too. Side by side. Like friends, right?*

It's three in the afternoon but Su-ae has still not returned.

All through cleaning the floor again, watering the orchids, and selling the occasional asters and rose bouquets, she looks out toward

Gwanghwamun or the Sejong Arts Center hoping to spot Su-ae, but for nothing. Hoping she might call, San stares at the phone but it doesn't ring. As she's gotten used to the work at the shop, the ritual has been a comfort. Putting their roots into pots, fertilizing them, and letting them grow as they would in the ground. As they grow green and tall, the plants soothe something inside of her. She used to pot them during the day, and at night she would come back to sit among them. That comfort is disappearing. As if removing tangles from her mind, she takes a moment to touch every single leaf of the plant before her. Where has the San from her first day of work gone? The one who would walk among the flowers and trees, whose lips would part slightly in wonder when she found a sprout she hadn't seen before or an unfamiliar plant tucked into a shelf corner? The one who took out the toolbox and hammered a nail to hang the watering can? Whose heart would fill up and cheeks turn red? She gently strokes each leaf of the weeping figs, sago palms, rubber figs, and orchids as she wipes away dust. Her handiwork as she places more moss into some of the pots is careful, but somehow unenthused. Each shriveled leaf is plucked out one by one.

Stretching her back, she goes up to the metal table. From the drawer she takes out a notepad, hairpins, and other belongings and puts them in a plastic bag. She adds the *Flower World* the man left. A business card drops to the floor and she bends over to pick it up. Her hand is about to place it in the card box but she finds herself staring at it instead. That man who always stared at her as if he might eat her up, the one who would habitually ask her out— Choi's card. Unconsciously, she also puts it into her plastic bag. Not realizing Su-ae has come in, San opens the last drawer and places a sweat-dried handkerchief into the bag as well.

"What are you doing," Su-ae demands.

"I'm sorry."

As San continues to put things into the plastic bag, Su-ae places some Styrofoam boxes on the desk.

"You haven't eaten, right? It's sushi."

San doesn't respond.

"I'm sorry I was mad."

"You had every right to be."

"If you really think that, you'll eat some sushi. All right?"

". . ."

"If you're going to collect your things here, do you want me to go to our apartment and pack up my things?"

"That's not the same."

"How is it different?"

". . ."

"I love this flower shop. I want to be with someone who loves plants. This flower shop is like my uncle. And I have so much I want to do in the future. I want to do it with you."

San doesn't respond.

"I wish we could talk about what we're thinking. How else are we going to comfort each other or support each other or whatever! God, look at me getting mad again. All right, let's eat our sushi first."

Su-ae is waiting for her to take a bite when suddenly San throws her head back. Blood drips down her upper lip. Grabbing a tissue, Su-ae quickly wipes the blood away, balls some tissue up to plug her nostril, and wets a towel to place on San's forehead.

"This won't do. You've got to go home and rest."

San tries to wave her hand no, but Su-ae shouts, "Stop it! Go rest at home. But I'm taking no prisoners tomorrow."

When the bleeding ceases, Su-ae gets San's things and a box of sushi together and puts them into San's hands. She practically shoves San out the door.

"You'll feel better after a nice long sleep, okay?"

Her anger is gone, and her face is concerned as she pushes San out the door. As soon as San steps outside, the sunlight makes her squint. It must be time for Paris Baguette to bake a new batch of bread; savory smells float in the air.

"Come on, go home."

When San looks back, Su-ae waves.

As she takes a few steps toward Gwanghwamun, carrying her bag and the box of sushi, Su-ae shouts after her, "San! I'll take no prisoners tomorrow!"

When San looks back, Su-ae smiles widely and waves again. But as San turns away again, Su-ae's face turns dark. She stands there in the door of the flower shop until San is out of sight.

With one foot on the first step into the underground passage, San seems to have second thoughts and turns back. Her cheeks have shrunken overnight, and her eyelids are trembling. Right before the entrance leading to Kyobo Bookstore are a pair of phone booths. Is she about to call someone? She slips into one of the booths. Taking out a phonecard from her bag, she inserts it and begins to dial a number before stopping midway.

A little later, she emerges from the booth without the box of sushi. Only her bag hangs from her shoulder. She doesn't go down the underground passage that leads toward the apartment but instead walks to the main street that leads from Gwanghwamun to Seodaemun. As she passes a shoe store, pharmacy, and tailor, she stops and walks back to the tailor specializing in trousers. Between the tailor and a bank, there's a bookstore. She looks intently at the window display. On a shelf is a copy of *Flower World*. She enters the store and takes a copy down from the shelf. The cover features a sunflower field. Were these sunflowers also photographed by the man? She looks inside the cover. The photo credit features the man's name. She stares at the name until the store owner asks, "Would you like it in a bag?"

Her hands, having lost Su-ae's sushi, now carry a paper tote with a copy of *Flower World* inside. She passes the land bridge and Bonjour Café to where the new art museum has been built on the former grounds of a high school. The ginkgo trees beyond the museum are yellow. In the empty lot, construction is still going on. Perhaps due to the sound, there are only a few people sitting here and there.

She collapses onto a bench.

What has drawn her here? The excavator is like a dinosaur with an open mouth as it plunges into the ground, and she keeps a close eye on the man controlling it. She stares until her neck feels stiff. The construction workers break. From the haze of dust, a group in red hard hats walk in her direction. They lean on the yellow iron railing or sit on the benches next to hers and drink coffee while giving her looks that seem to say, What's up with her, as she continues to stare at the excavator.

"What's she looking at?"

"I think she's not right in the head?"

"Some country mouse."

"Better than the sluts they have around here."

"Don't start."

One of the men explodes in laughter.

Laughter or not, she continues to stare at the excavator. No doubt some of the men are making fun of her. Having ceased digging, the excavator raises its teeth to the sky and soaks in the autumn sunlight.

She just about manages to turn her gaze to the museum grounds. Where the two women playing badminton had been, their skirts stopping short of their knees, there is only sun bouncing off the earth. Ignoring the jeers of the men around her, she gets up and crosses the lot. The violets she planted—where the man might look down from his office building—the ones she planted with her face burning from the mere thought of him—those flowers have wilted.

Even their leaves, since they were exposed to such harsh sunlight. She looks around. She can't find what she's looking for, and her face falls. Walking toward the outdoor taps, she suddenly has a change of heart and turns around. Outside the museum grounds, she buys two one-liter bottles of drinking water. She opens the caps and waters the parched violets. She tries spreading each shriveled leaf with her hands but the violets will not revive. After pouring all the water, she slowly walks to the taps to fill up the empty bottles and waters the dried violets again. Her work is anxious but also lifeless. After the watering, she sits in the empty lot and stares at the dying plants. They look like they never possessed lush purple blossoms. Then, occasionally, she looks up at the building the man works in. The plastic bottles slip from her hand and roll about on the ground. The construction workers lose interest as she simply sits there, and they lapse into bored chatter.

Suddenly, when it seems as if she might sit there forever, San springs to her feet. By the time she's marched out of the lot, past the trees, and out onto the street, the copy of *Flower World* is no longer in her hand. There's just her bag hanging precariously from her shoulder. As if pushed, she ends up, once more, across the street from the building. Unlike before when she would hesitate, she crosses swiftly with the other pedestrians as soon as the signal changes. She barges into the café, puts her bag down in one of the chairs, and then goes to the phone booth next to the entrance to the bathroom. Inserting her phonecard, she rapidly dials the man's number. The bell rings, and she hears the word "Hello," his voice carrying over the line.

"Hello?"

"It's me, Oh San."

"What?"

"I'm in the café on the ground floor, can you come down for a second?"

"Who did you say you were?"

"Oh San."

"Wait a minute, let me square away some things here . . . Did you say your name was Oh San?"

"Yes."

". . . I'll be there in a second."

She puts down the receiver and goes back to where she put her bag. The San from the other day that hesitated about calling the man, sure that he would mock her, is gone.

Twenty minutes later, the man stands in front of her.

"Are you Oh San?"

She gets up. When the man sits down across from her, she returns to her seat.

Oh.

The man doesn't recognize her at all.

"I'm sorry, but I'm not quite sure why you've come to see me."

When she realizes he doesn't know who she is, her eyes widen in devastation. The man looks taken aback. He's trying hard to remember who she is but he truly can't. The devastation deepens. This past summer, this man had spoken as if making an important life discovery. *Look, I have something to say.* This very man.

The man seems to give up, and thinking that he might make a bigger mistake if he goes on trying to remember, instead sits up straight.

"So why did you want to see me?"

Suddenly, she pushes away her water and puts her face down in her arms. The man's complete failure to recognize her brings shocked tears to her eyes. She tries not to be caught crying and tries to keep her shoulders from heaving but soon sobs leak out of her in waves. Her effort to keep it all in makes her crying all the more dramatic.

The server, who has approached with a menu, simply backs off.

Surprised himself, the man keeps saying, Hey, hey, as he taps her shoulders. The more he does that, the more her shoulders heave. "Look, just say something. If you just burst into tears like this, what's everyone going to think of me?" After a few more attempts that turn to nothing, he looks down at her shoulders. What should he do? He glances out the large windows with an expression of puzzlement more than anything else, and leaves the café.

A little later, she's out on the street as well.

Her face is swollen from crying. The shock from not being recognized has left her senses tingling, and every little thing makes her jump.

She convinced herself she was wearing a sleeveless silk blouse that day. A plum-colored, sleeveless silk blouse, and that her arms had little goosebumps, and he nonchalantly said, *You must be cold*, and swept her arm, which, yes, had been desire. A desire that failed to disperse into mere memory, instead growing greener and thicker all summer, then rose up and led her to neglect. The unspent desire that infused her body with sadness was already overwhelming enough. But to have him look her in the eye and not recognize her—that was breaking her down.

Now she enters another café and calls someone else.

Not the photographer but Choi, the regular at the flower shop. She holds his business card. Choi always looks at her as if he's about to eat her. The receiver to her ear, she carefully states her location so Choi knows exactly where she is and adds:

"I just happened to be passing by. So I thought, maybe we could have some coffee?"

She hangs up and immediately regrets what she's done. This duality of the heart. Feeling depressed, she clutches her hands together.

Forgotten that night, has he? That night, how I shivered because all I was wearing was the plum-colored silk blouse, the cold breeze running goosebumps up my arm?

She's unaware that Choi has sat down across from her, so intent on staring at her own fingers. Choi reaches out and taps her shoulder. It's a little tap, but she almost falls backward before recovering her balance.

"What's with the hair? I almost didn't recognize you."

On the pocket of Choi's white shirt is a spot of ink. Miffed by her overreaction, Choi follows her gaze to the spot.

"What, this? My fountain pen wasn't working so I shook it a bit. The ink splattered. Hell, bad luck to get it on here."

She laughs, and Choi perks up.

"You're prettier when you laugh. Wanna kiss?"

"Hmph!"

"Careful, you might drop some snot."

As if she really has, San rubs the end of her nose with her hand. Choi has that look on his face again. He lights a cigarette. She's only seen him at the flower shop until now; he looks like a different person outside of it.

"But what's up? You've never done this before. When I ask you out to dinner you act like a Buddhist nun. What about tonight?"

"I have to go play badminton!"

The ridiculous answer just pops out of her mouth. Badminton? Surprise at her own words makes her eyes widen.

"Badminton?"

Saying this word makes the cigarette drop from his lips and roll off the table onto the floor. When Choi bends to pick it up, the inky spot on his white pocket twists in an ugly manner.

The man who sat across from her and might as well have said, I'm sorry, who are you? It's just that my memory is bad, and my eyesight even worse . . . The man who stared as the devastation made her cry.

196

Had she cried?

She slowly bites down on her lip.

The man said, *So why did you want to see me*—did she throw a cup of water on the floor, put her head down on the table, and cry?

Her unexpected desire lanced through the sunlight and the green plants, through the dream of never being bothered by anyone in a large room of her own with a wide table. Desire for this man would wake her up in the middle of the night, washing away her childhood feelings of loss and abandonment. Even sweeping aside the moment with Namae before the sea of minari, filling up the emptiness inside her.

The sandcastle she built has crumbled in the face of his careless words.

San finally realizes calling Choi was a mistake. Unwilling to bear another second, she jumps up from her seat and runs away as fast as she can. But Choi follows her out and grabs her wrist, hard. He's staring at her with an aggressive look she's never seen before.

"I'm sorry!"

"For what?"

She suddenly comes to her senses. She recognizes the hunger Choi is exuding.

"I know what girls like you want."

"No! You're wrong!"

Choi drags her to some steps leading into a basement. She struggles, but Choi is strong. She has to escape; she has to assuage his hunger. All she can hear is the sound of panting.

"Let me go, please!"

"So why did you call me? With that sad expression of yours. And now you want me to let you go? You've got the wrong guy for that. Do you think that's what I'm going to do? Come on. Relax. It's no fun if you're all tense. This is an emergency exit. Unless the elevator breaks down, no one is going to come by. And so what if a couple of people see you? Isn't it more fun with an audience?"

Choi pushes her to the edge of the stairway and snatches her skirt. In desperation, she bites down on his shoulder. He makes a fist and punches her in the face.

"Stop that!"

She tries to slap him but Choi grabs her wrist and twists her arm. She closes her eyes. The ceiling and stairs breathe shallowly and close in on her. As her strength leaves her slightly, Choi loosens his grip a little and touches her lips. She keeps her lips firmly closed. When she refuses to open her mouth no matter how much he digs with his fingers, Choi gets angry and forces her against the wall. Her skirt is ripped off and tossed to the floor.

"Let's not do this here—a room . . . Take me to a room, at least—"

"If you hadn't run, that's what I was about to do. A nice dinner, a glass of wine, dancing somewhere with a view of the river, I was going to do all that. But you seem a little desperate. So I got a little rough. But this isn't too bad either, right? I wish you'd cooperate a little more . . . You're like this now but tomorrow you'll be calling me again. Saying you're waiting for me here. It's written on your face. Hey, you've committed no sin. All I'm doing is what you can't bear to ask for—come on, do as I say."

She tries to turn her head away from his breath but he twists her head so they're face to face again. Squirming away from the lips against her neck only makes Choi grip her harder. His hands roughly grope for her breasts and squeeze them. His lips push into her mouth. Every attempt to resist is met with his greater strength. In a moment, her head begins to droop.

She's released into the street.

Her mind is completely taken over, her body a husk. No one seems to take note of the loneliness she carries. Just some woman in the crowd, unaware that her top is undone. A more observant person might have noticed her ear and cheek slightly swollen from having been punched, the thin lines of her face a touch asymmetrical because of it. Someone might see her pale face and think, How could anyone ever look so pale . . . Is she going to fall? And look back for a moment to see if she does. But that's the extent of the interest she inspires as other pedestrians overtake her. The lone button keeping her shirt together will soon drop to the ground. But she will probably keep walking without noticing anyway. At least the button keeps her clothes on for now. With every step, it rubs itself against her heart underneath where it hurts. When she walks in between the buildings, sunlight hits the button and turns it gold. She is dazed at first, but soon her limp steps gain a little stiffness, bringing on strong chills that make her want to stop.

Where she does finally stop is the art museum. This is where she decides never to return to the flower shop or the long room again. As darkness falls, the empty lot takes on a fearsome air. The smoking construction workers are gone. There's just the earth-eating dinosaur of the excavator, stoically regarding the ghostlike San. She passes the wooden bench where she sat that afternoon, and goes up to the railing where the construction workers joked in their tired voices. She picks up a cigarette butt. What do I do with this, her perplexed expression says, before she puts it between her lips and pretends to take an exhausted drag. Su-ae's face as she takes a delicious drag while at the farm. It was right there. Last summer in the midafternoon, two women playing badminton in short denim skirts, aware of the construction workers' eyes. San's gaze caresses the spot.

She remembers clearly thinking that her sadness might kill her one day. In the face of the hate thrown at her before she'd even had the chance to ask if the girl loved her—the only thing to do was to die. Only my death can make her love me. And if I have to die, I'll die right here. The thought of sitting down before the wild minari field and chanting, If I have to die someday, I will die right here, if it means making you love me, if I could make you love me then I will die—that has been the only thing, day to day, that has allowed her to endure anyway.

Having pretended to smoke, she suddenly seems confused and tosses away the cigarette butt. The excavator stands before her. San walks slowly toward it. What a lot of earth it's gone through. It has removed piles and piles of soil. It stands there in the flower bed she made like some satiated beast. She searches the ground around it; no sign of the violets. Just an empty water bottle rolling about her feet. The flowers she had planted one by one have been turned over in a single moment and are gone. *Ahh—ak—* Her screams echo against the piles of earth and the walls of the art museum, resounding through the trees along the street, but no one hears. Only San herself, as it bounces against the museum and comes back to her in the dark. It makes Choi's blow throb enough to split. When her heart felt empty, she would try to listen carefully to what sound it made; now all that overflows in her ears is her scream. Violet. Violence. Violator . . . With all her might she scratches the excavator with her nails. It does nothing to the machine. Despite her scratching at it with all ten fingers, the excavator remains oblivious and all that breaks are her nails. She makes two fists and beats down on the machine. It only makes her hands bleed. This time, she closes her eyes and smashes her face against it. It only breaks her nose. Violet. Violence. Violator . . . She's throwing every part of her body at it now. Not pushing, but smashing herself against it. Taking a few steps back and running into it. Another few steps back and running into it, harder. The excavator doesn't budge. Her resistance doesn't leave the slightest damage. Only she is getting bloodied in the process. As if staring into a vast abyss, she gazes into the machine's mouth before throwing off her shoes and struggling to climb it. Her bag dangles from her shoulder. Her shin hits steel and makes a breaking sound, and as she crawls, a metal edge rips the flesh of her breast. Swallowing the blood flowing from a burst lip, her elbow smashes on another edge. But she doesn't seem to be in pain. She is hanging on to the side of the imposing and indestructible main body of the excavator, making her way inch by inch to its open maw. Her skirt's hook, ripped by Choi, finally gives way and her skirt slides off her waist. The button that held her front together also drops off, and her shirt opens, fluttering in the breeze. Her blunt black haircut is a tangled mess. The maw is half-full of earth from the underworld. Letting out a sigh, she places her bleeding, wounded feet into that earth. Her expression is one of relief. As she brings up scoops of earth to cover her knees, thighs, and hips, she even laughs a little.

You forgot who I was?

My arm in that sleeveless plum-colored silk blouse, the tiny goosebumps, the way you swept them away. You forgot that. What can I do that will make you remember?

When she runs out of earth to bury herself in, she stares up at the stars. A memory of the man's face as he failed to recognize her threatens to make her shake again. But the crisis passes. As she thinks how she can't go back to who she was yesterday, or even who she was that morning, her body finally begins to feel like it belongs to her.

She sits in the maw of the excavator on the museum grounds.

When Su-ae's face appears in the night sky, a brief spark of life flashes in her eyes. But they go out of focus once more. Too short and empty a spark. Is she unconscious? She's doing nothing now but dozing. Once in a while, her shoulder jerks and she gives a start. This must be around when the blood from her torn breast has dried a bit, and the iron smell from that wound has faded. She tries hard to open her eyes. Maybe she's thinking that if she could get down, she could go visit her mother. Poor mother. I know how unhappy you were. I can do what you want now. But she can't find the strength. The smell of blood from her wounds mixes with the perfume of the night air and dissipates into the eerie art museum. It looks like she's trying to open her eyes again, but they close. Blood from her torn forehead flows like tears across her cheek, drying there. Around the time the stars begin disappearing, the last thing she has done in her grave is to wrap one hand around her damaged elbow, rummage through her bag, take out her notebook, open it to a random page, and try to press down some letters, only to find that it is too much.

Before It Gets Dark

In December, a tall Christmas tree goes up at City Hall Plaza. Right before six, its lights are turned on all at once. From Deoksugung Palace all the way to Gyeongbokgung Palace, the bare ginkgo trees are also decorated with twinkling lights. Large crowds wait for the lights to change, crossing when the signal turns green. At lunchtime or around dinner, the restaurants and cafés fill with people. Most of the seats by the windows are reserved. Pomodoro Restaurant, where two young women ate from time to time, has long lines of customers waiting to order spaghetti and garlic bread. The vendor where San bought a hairband on her birthday is now selling miniature Christmas trees for tabletops or balconies. These dark green trees sport little golden and silver stars as well as a Santa Claus doll hanging on top. Looking a little closer, a new wine store seems to have opened next to Pomodoro. Its glass door advertises specially priced French wine, two bottles for ₩9,900. Her hands in the pockets of her coat, a young woman with lips blue from the cold glances at the red letters and enters the store. And is it because of Pomodoro's influence? The old noodle place that crafted tiny, delicious dumplings has remodeled, changed their sign, and is now a pasta spot called Gio. There's a Christmas tree in its window.

Just another day near the end of the year.

The photographer, whose camera took photos of violets in the summer, is seen walking into the flower store. The store has changed. The blue buckets always out on the pavement are now crammed inside. The buckets brim with baby's breath, red roses, lilies, and carnations. Blinking fairy lights frame the window. The farm owner is there alone, and he gets up to greet the photographer. The radio channel is set to 89.1 FM, and a DJ says, Have you seen the movie *Buena Vista Social Club*? I'm sure many of you had heard the music before you saw the movie. In Korean, the title means "a social club where you're welcomed," which sounds like a lovely name for a record.

The photographer has come in with an assignment on narcissi. Apparently this was planned, because while the photographer prepares his equipment, the farm owner goes straight to the narcissus buckets, takes out a tied bunch, undoes the knot, and begins to construct a bouquet.

The man asks, "They say the narcissus is the flower that goes best with white snow; why is that?"

The farm owner looks at him as if to say, I don't know, and in silence positions the narcissi this way and that so the photographer can see it from various angles. A tall glass vase is brought out and they place the blooms inside for more photos. As he's about to take the picture, the man suddenly seems to remember something and looks around the flower shop. Looking for someone. His gaze travels around the sago palms, rubber figs, ficus bonsai, weeping figs, and lady palms. As if there is someone among the trees. Is he remembering how he came to this shop to take photographs of violets? He seems to be looking for the woman who worked in silence, her gaze lowered, helping him get the best shot of the unassuming purple flowers. Her gentle, peaceful movements. His gaze glides past the crocuses, moschatels, and ferns, turning wistful. He's suddenly remembered that early autumn day when a woman came to see him where he worked, who buried her face and burst into tears. The face of the strange, crying girl in the café finally super-imposes itself on the face of the shop employee with the beautiful eyelashes. If they were the same woman, why had she suddenly come to him and burst into tears? He puts his camera down and brings the pen and paper toward him. He writes to the farm owner:

The woman who works here, where is she?

The farm owner puts down the narcissus in his hand, takes the pen, and writes his answer next to the man's question.

She's on vacation.

The man writes once more.

In the middle of winter?

The farm owner hesitates. He's about to write something but gives up. The man writes once more.

What's her name?

The farm owner writes next to this question that her name is Lee Su-ae, his niece. The man writes, *Oh really? I didn't know.* He is about to pick up his camera when instead, he writes once more.

But where did she go on vacation?

Thinking for a moment, the farm owner slowly begins to write.

She is not actually on vacation. That girl likes to run off from time to time. An old habit. She is an unhappy child. One summer day, her vacationing family was in a ravine when there was a flash flood, and only she survived. She pretends to be strong and cold but she is actually sensitive and vulnerable. Sometimes she goes off and comes back. Once she didn't come back for two years. Now it's not so long. She's always back after four or five days. It's a bit long this time. About a week already. But she'll be back. She loves this flower shop very much. Do you know Su-ae well?

The man takes over.

No, I don't. She helped me take the photos of the violets this summer; I wanted to say hello.

The farm owner looks at him strangely, and bows his head as he writes.

You don't mean Su-ae; you mean that other girl.

The man looks at the farm owner as if to ask, That other girl?

She looked after things at the shop this summer. The one who helped you with the violets isn't Su-ae but her. She's . . .

The farm owner grips the pen and is lost in his thoughts for a moment before he sighs and writes on.

Something bad seems to have happened to her. She left the apartment she lived in with Su-ae and never came back. Leaving all her clothes and notebooks and books and her bag.

In Samcheong-dong still is the apartment with traces of the young woman. The carnivorous plant, the shriveled herbs, notebooks, a few books, a bag, some cups, a fountain pen, and hairpins. Dull-colored clothes, low-heeled shoes, and the minifridge she used as a desk to write blue letters in her notebook the day she got her job at the flower shop, pleasure spreading across her face. And the single, unopened letter that arrived after she was gone.

Did something happen to her?

Well, it's difficult to say. I don't quite know myself. She just disappeared one day and did not come back. A patient and hardworking girl, and a generous personality. Su-ae loved having her around. She was a quiet young woman and a very diligent worker. We have to find someone else now.

What was her name?

Oh San.

Silence flows between the two men. Through it, the radio pipes up again. How was that? Wasn't it a truly beautiful and moving song? You've just heard one of the songs from *Buena Vista Social Club*, written by Wim Wenders and Ry Cooder. Doesn't it hit you right in the heart? The level of attention these old greats bring to their music is really intense. They do it not for anyone else but for their own enjoyment, and I suppose that's how it's possible. People for whom music is life and life is music. Let me translate some of the lines for you. *I want to hide my pain from the flowers. I don't want to tell them of life's suffering. Because if they know my sadness, the flowers will cry too.*

Oh San.

Melancholy, the man looks outside at the parking lot. He is standing right where she used to sprinkle water on the glass. There's a recital by a famous violinist that evening, and the parking lot has its NO VACANCY sign up. Remembering something, the man rummages through his bag until he finds an envelope he seems to have carried around for a long time. It's stamped with the Kodak logo, and it's the photo he's looking for: it's her, San. From before her desire. As if some memory is coming back to life, he stares forcefully at the picture. That summer day, when she lowered her eyes as she looked at the violets. He's remembering how the rain had passed and the sun was shining outside the shop, how he suddenly felt a wave of tedium as he took photos of the violets. He's remembering what he discovered then, when her thick eyelashes threw delicate shadows on her face. Back then he didn't suppress his disappointment at the camera's failure to elevate the lowly violets, and the sight of her eyelashes was as exciting as fresh dew. It was only this past summer when his disappointment spurred him to photograph her eyelashes. But he still seems uncertain as to whether this is the same woman who was at the café in his office building and had burst into tears.

He puts the photos down on the table.

If you ever see her again, give her these pictures.

As he takes more photos of the yellow narcissi, the woman in the photo remains on the steel desk. Finally, just as she fervently wished, the woman is a hair's breadth away from the man. *Don't wake me up, they are all sleeping. Gladioli and white lilies. I don't want my sadness to be known to the flowers. If they see my tears they will die.* Having finished his work, the man puts his camera away. He says his goodbyes to the farm owner and walks out the door of the shop, cold wind making his shirttails flutter. Inside the flower shop, the farm owner takes a look at the photographs. Her eyelashes lowered as she looks at the violets, from the front, from the side, just after she looks up, again when she looks back down. Waving her hand at the lens, Please stop. Of the photos, the farm owner looks the longest at the one from the side.

The photographer tucks in his shirttails and takes a few steps away, but then turns back to the shop window. On the glass door decorated with fairy lights, there's a small sign that reads *Wanted: A woman to look after flowers.* He is staring at this sign when someone shoves past him to enter. It's Choi. The farm owner puts the photographs away. When the photographer finally turns away, Choi is choosing plants to send to an end-of-year event. Writing down the message to be put on the banner. The photographer walks on and goes into a café with a window looking out onto the street. He sits by this window, orders coffee, lights a cigarette, and stares out at the pale gray scene. Later he stands on the pavement as the sun shines down, his camera bag on his shoulder. The streets are crowded. He passes what was Nonjang Bookstore, now a liquor store, and a boutique and a watchmaker. Across from Koryo Supermarket is Café La Muse where he and San happened to bump into each other, where now people look down from the windows as the man walks by bumping shoulders with other pedestrians. He walks the street where San left behind countless footsteps, lost in her thoughts of him; the streets keep changing as if to erase every trace of her. There's a new parking lot near Gyeonghuimun, and a new marinated-crab restaurant called Mir in the next alley. Café Bonjour has changed its sign, declaring itself a restaurant, and in the Hengeuk Life Insurance building, an art cinema called

Cinecube has opened. On its ground floor is a new French restaurant called Russian. The building has a little fountain as well as wooden benches and a small grove of bamboo. Next to the art museum, where the ravenous excavator used to be, ready to destroy all and everything, is a new building. This building, with its countless windows, now blocks the view of the taps where San gathered water in plastic bottles. It is impossible to tell where exactly San planted her white, yellow, purple, and pink violets. An embattled-looking conscript on leave is standing at a stationery street vendor, choosing a new notebook. A middle-aged man drops a ₩10,000 note into a Salvation Army kettle. From the cinema on the street to Jeong-dong leading to Pauline Books and Changdeok Girls' Middle School, youths are pouring out under the darkening sky. A young woman who has lost her party is looking around as the lights blink on one by one. San is no longer on these streets. Past Saemoonan Church and Gyeonghuimun, the man adjusts his camera bag once more, rubs his face with his palms, and walks toward the traffic light in front of Samsung Hospital. As the light changes, the man crosses the street. His back, among the crowds of people who come and go, soon moves out of sight.

The Return of the "Little Girl"

Recently, I took *Violets* down from the shelf and read it again. Memories of my younger self began to resurface. At the time of writing the novel, I was suffering from migraines that felt like an awl jabbing my brain and necessitated that I take painkillers first thing in the morning. A president heralded as a symbol of democracy was in power then, but the streets of Seoul were filled with protesters vehemently opposing his administration. It was a time when women and stories of women were being systemically discriminated against and silenced.

One day, on a walk in an attempt to alleviate the pain, I sat down on a park bench in the middle of the city and saw two young women playing badminton in a nearby empty lot. Behind them was a construction site with a looming excavator, an enormous heap of earth in its claw. It looked ready to swallow the two women whole. This sight unsettled me. By the time I came home, I had an idea for a novel. One about a "little girl" who eventually finds work in the middle of the city, at a flower shop. To go on this journey with her, I worked on a farm in Gupabal for six months myself, taking care of trees and flowers. Mysteriously enough, once I began working on the farm and writing this book, my migraines vanished.

The first line of this novel is: "A little girl." Never celebrated or welcomed in the small rural village of her birth, and self-isolating after a traumatic childhood experience, she nevertheless has the desire to write and tell her story that sprouts within her. This is the story of a woman unable to find a place to fit in the world, suddenly swept up into a warped desire for love that eventually breaks her; it is the story of a woman punished by violent men in a cruel city because she is unable to express her confused desire for love and connection, who then disappears into the dark. After I finished the first draft of *Violets*, I watched the documentary *Buena Vista Social Club* alone at a cinema. I can't explain the connection between my novel and this film, but I found myself coming home from the theater and sitting down at my desk, rewriting the ending of my manuscript.

Violets are very small plants. So small, they're easily overlooked as weeds. That's why I decided on the title *Violets*. There are women all around us who exist in silence, anonymous and without anything special about them; she could be me and she could be you. To amplify the voices of those women, whom no one could hear unless one was listening very carefully, to let them speak through my words — this is *Violets*. San eventually leaves this cruel city, but I also wanted to hint she was still a persistent witness from somewhere with her eyes wide open. After being violated, she drags her broken body to the maw of an excavator at a nighttime construction site. I wanted there to be a single moment where an anonymous and unremarkable woman would confront a staunch and immovable violence head-on. As a writer, what I could do for this woman was to have her take out her notebook in the darkness, amid this violence, and write. I believed only then could her story be returned to her, and to us.

I do not think my belief was in vain.

I am no longer as young as I was when I wrote *Violets*. But the "little girl," after having long faded away, has returned, thanks to the skillful hands of my translator. He tells me he cried as he translated *Violets*; this moved me. Because I, too, cried a long time ago as I wondered, *Who will ever understand what is trapped in the heart of this "little girl"?* I hope she now finds understanding in your hearts as well—that she may, after her loneliness and isolation, walk forth into the light.

—Kyung-Sook
Autumn 2021